Distant Thunder

CHIP'S DIARY

BARBARA M. LAMACCHIA

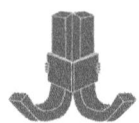

Double J Press
Berlin, Massachusetts
Copyright © Barbara Lamacchia 2024

All rights reserved. No part of this book may be reproduced or transmitted in any form or by any means, electronic, or mechanized, including photocopying, recording, or by any information storage and retrieval system without the written permission of the publisher and/or author, except as provided by U.S. Copyright Law.

ISBN 979-8-9903879-1-1 (paperback)
ISBN 979-8-9903879-0-4 (ebook)
Library of Congress Control Number: 2024905878

Book Cover Design and Interior Formatting by 100Covers.

For Tommy

Who remains an American classic to those of us who enjoyed the pleasure of his company, laughed with him, loved him.

KERR FAMILY TREE

Robert Kerr — Theresa Dennehy

Moira (Mimi) m. Neil Mullaney	Cecilia (Cissy) m. Carl Davenport	John (Pup) m. Elaine Sanborn	Sheila (Gabby) m. Stanley Zeresky	Dennis (Champ) Deceased	Daniel (Chip) m. Rosalina Arroyo	Bridget (Bridy)	Elizabeth (Biddy) m. Dexter Weintraub
Patrick	Michael	Chase	Dylan		Bryant Wilson, Jr.		
Fiona	Matthew	Jared	Madison		Marla Wilson		
Maeve							
Aiden							
Brendan							
Shannon							
Liam							

Chapter 1

1985

The yellowed notebook caught the man's eye as he rummaged through a trunk in his attic. The spiral bound notebook looked vaguely familiar, but it was not until the man opened the book, its pages crinkly with age, did the man remember. Dan (Chip) Kerr smiled over his long-ago creation and sat on the trunk to read.

In those days, Dan had plenty to write about since he was one of eight Kerr kids. His life was a constant whirl of family, school, and church. The boy at the time did not know the meaning of boredom. Nor did he lack events or activities to write about or comment on.

His life seemed like high drama fraught with exciting climaxes and tension. The real-life characters who peopled his diary, like his Great Aunt Julia with her acid tongue, or his siblings with their many quirks, gave him plenty of material. His bad boy cousins, Anthony and Girard, were perfect juvenile villains. The kids at school provided abundant humor and pathos unique to sixth graders. Dan settled himself and began to read:

My name is Dan Kerr aka Chip as I'm known to my family and close friends. I've just begun the sixth grade at St. Thomas Aquinas School. My journal will begin with last Fourth of July and I'll write about my life until next year's Fourth. Before I get to last summer's events, I will write about the early days of this school year.

I can tell this year will be the best of my long school experience. My teacher is Sister Ursula, who is young and enthusiastic, and she loves writing, vocabulary, and reading. Already she has started what she calls Word of the Week. Each week fifteen kids, chosen by Sister, have to look up a word, write the definition, and explain and the use of the word in a sentence to be written on the board. The rest of the class must write down the word, definition, and sentence. We will be quizzed the following week.

The word I've chosen is actually two words, grass widow. *I looked it up, but I couldn't find it anywhere. I still don't know what it means but it sounds too good to just throw away. I overheard my mother using the words and I loved the sound of them.*

My work is done, and I can't stop picturing the reaction to my words when I put them on the board today. Before that happens, I have to get through religion, math, history, and geography. English is just before lunch. Most of what we did in the first four classes was lost on me, which is unusual. I love school; it's just that I'm so excited for English that I couldn't really concentrate on anything else. I'll just copy Saba's notes and ask him to explain whatever I don't quite get.

The time came. As usual, Chatty Cathy's hand was in the air first when Sister asked for volunteers to go to the board. Her word is insipid. *That has got to be the dumbest word in the English language. No surprise that Chatty Cathy chose it. She is one of the dumbest humans in the human race, an opinion shared by everyone but her, of course. A few more people went up before I raised my hand and practically ran to the board where I wrote my sentence in my best Palmer penmanship,*

"My Aunt Julia, a grass widow, lives in New York."

There were two kids before me who had to explain their words, but I know mine is still the best. The class was just beginning to realize what I'd written because I saw some pointing and heard some whispering. Then I heard some quiet laughing. Dopes. They didn't know a good word when they saw one.

"Daniel, please read and explain your word for us," says Sister.

"Yes, Sister. 'My Aunt Julia, a grass widow, lives in New York.'"

Suddenly I realized I didn't have a clue what to say. Seconds passed and I felt sweat at the roots of my hair. I had no choice but to look to Sister for help. She knew I don't know and asked the class, "What do you think grass widow means?"

Kenny Johnson's hand was immediately in the air.

"Yes, Kenneth. What do you think it means?"

"Well, Sister. Maybe the woman's husband was a snake in the grass, and he died and now she's a grass widow."

"Interesting explanation," said Sister. "Anyone else?"

Chatty Cathy was about to inform us. "Sister, I know what it means, but I don't think I should say it."

"Then don't." Sister snapped. We all stared at Sister, stunned by her tone. Chatty Cathy sunk back to her seat with one leg under her. Had I been in my right mind, I would have pointed out to Sister Chatty Cathy's unladylike position in her chair, and Chatty Cathy would have been practicing sitting like a lady after school.

"What Daniel has written is called an archaic expression," said Sister. "You don't need to write that down. It's a term you'll learn in a few years. Daniel, you may take your seat."

I returned to my seat embarrassed and mad.

Time for recess. I would rather stay in the room, but I know I couldn't. Sister returned from her lunch and watched everyone file silently out of the classroom. As I passed her, she said quietly. "Daniel, wait a minute. Why did you choose a word that you knew you couldn't explain?"

"I thought it sounded good," I mumbled.

"Where did you hear it?"

"From my mother."

Sister smiled. "Do you really have an Aunt Julia?"

"Yes. My mother was talking about her, and I liked what she said."

Sister smiled again. "I guess that your mother wouldn't like it if she knew you were quoting her in front of the class."

"She doesn't know that I overheard what she said."

"When I said that it's an archaic expression, I meant that people really don't use this expression anymore. It means that your Aunt Julia is divorced."

DIVORCED? Did she say divorced? Someone in my family? Oh my God. Oh my God. No wonder Mum stopped talking as soon as she saw me. What an idiot I am. And I didn't even thank Sister for saving me from making an even bigger idiot of myself in front of the class.

"I'm sorry, Sister. I'll make sure I know what my word means the next time I have to do this."

Sister smiled again. "Lesson learned?" she asked.

"Yes, Sister."

"You better get outside. You're missing recess."

"Where have you been, Kerr? I've been waiting for you forever." Saba was mad.

"I was talking to Sister. I didn't want to come out. Did anyone say anything?"

Saba smiled. *"Of course, Dello Russo started but I threatened to rearrange his face and that was the end of that. Nobody else said a word. I think Chubs did the same thing and told off Davison and Winkler. You pulled a real boneheaded play this time, Kerr."*

And Saba was right, but no one said a word about my stupidity.

Now that I've started my journal, I can take the time to see my life for what it is. My world revolves around family, school, and church. I live with my parents and seven brothers and sisters in what my grandmother calls the "Kerr Compound." She says if the Kennedys can have their compound in Hyannis Port, we Kerrs can have ours in Coltonwood. Both sets of grandparents live on the same street as my family. My mother's parents, Dennis and Nellie (Keating) Dennehy, live on the corner at one end of the street while my father's parents, John and Margaret (Moriarty) Kerr, live five houses down from us at the other end of School Street.

All of us kids have family nicknames; we never call each other by our real names. The oldest is Moira (Mimi); she's twenty-two and engaged to Neil Mullaney. They are getting married next spring. Next is Cecilia (Cissy) who is twenty and not engaged to anyone. I call the two of them the drama queens because they have so many different methods to get their way. I'm so glad Mimi will be out of my hair in a few months. My oldest brother is John (Pup). Our neighbor, Mrs. Salina, named him Pup since he was always in trouble for one reason or another. Pup is eighteen and a senior in high school. He's planning to go into the Marines after he graduates. Sheila is sixteen. Her nickname is Gabby, not because she talks too much, but too little. She's my favorite sister, who has no trouble talking to me. My brother Dennis (Champ) is thirteen. He got his nickname because he's so good at sports. He plays baseball, football, and basketball. He's a terrible student but he thinks it doesn't matter since he's sure he will be signed by some big-league team before he finishes high school. Bridget (Bridy) is eight and a pest. When she's not in school, she spends all her time at home coloring on the living room floor in front of the tv. She hates being outside except in the winter when she can skate. The youngest is Elizabeth (Biddy). She's five and too cute for words. This is the opinion of several adults who know her. She's ok, but she's the baby and takes advantage, big time.

My Dad owns his own business, Bert's TV - Sales and Service. He also sells radios and record players and stereos. Dad learned about electronics when he was a radioman in the Army during WWII. After the war, he worked odd jobs and started dating his neighbor who became his wife. He borrowed some money from his father to start a business selling radios. As tv became more popular, he began repairing and then selling them. Eventually he rented a store on Main St. and expanded the business to almost exclusively sales.

We tried to get Dad to sell records, but he said he didn't want a bunch of kids hanging around the store. I guess he had a point, but he could make a lot of money selling records and albums. The drama queens and Gabby could keep him in business.

Coltonwood is a small city some twenty miles west of Boston. It was founded as a settlement during the days when there were Indian tribes living in the area. It eventually became a town and then a city when the population grew when all the Irish, Italian, and French immigrants found work and stayed.

The main street is home to a lot of old buildings that I love to explore with my friend Bobby. Some of the buildings are really nice with marble floors and stairs with a lot of polished wood. Most of these *buildings are now doctors' and dentists' and lawyers' offices. City hall is the best building. I love the smell of the old wood. Bobby and I never talk when we are exploring city hall. It seems that it's a building like a church or a library where you have to be quiet.*

Bobby Salina is my best neighborhood friend. He goes to the public school so he's not one of my school friends. He has three older sisters. His mother is a riot. She's Italian and speaks good English unless she can't think of a word in English, and she will say it in Italian. Bobby's father is a carpenter and makes his own wine. He also built a skating rink in their backyard for the whole neighborhood to use.

I've lived here my whole life. I can't imagine living anywhere else or going to any other school. My life is good so writing the journal will be fun. I think.

Nostalgic remembrance washed over Dan as he finished reading his journal. He stood and stretched and remembered that he was in the attic to clean, not to read. Hastily, he moved some boxes around so he could later tell himself he did some work. Dan didn't need to worry that Rosalina would check; she refused to set foot in the attic for any reason. The attic was full of Kerr junk; nothing that was of any interest to her.

Dan was startled when his wife called up to him. "How are you doing up there? It sounds pretty quiet to me."

"Just a minute. I'm coming down."

Dan descended the ladder that hung precariously above the bedroom ceiling. He shoved it back into place with some effort.

Rosalina faced him, arms akimbo. "Well, how much did you accomplish?"

"Not much. I found an old diary and I couldn't resist reading it."

"You kept a diary?" Rosalina was not successful in keeping amusement from her voice.

"I wrote this when I was in the sixth grade," Dan explained. "At the time, I was convinced that I was going to be a bestselling author so decided to keep a journal for a whole year. I really believed that I would one day win a Pulitzer Prize."

"I'd like to read it. I'll bet you revealed a lot about yourself without knowing it. May I read it?"

"Sure. I do want to read it one more time."

Rosalina didn't wait for Dan to finish. She took it upon herself to read the diary whenever she could. Questions came as soon as she finished the first installment.

"Dan, is the Dello Russo you mentioned in the diary the same guy who was a pallbearer at your brother's funeral?"

"Yup. Same guy. It's terrible what happened to Mike. He gave his all to serve his country now he's generally regarded as a lowlife, an unambitious vagrant. It's so unfair that his hometown gives him so little respect. It's not right."

"Were you friendly with him in school?"

"Kind of. We weren't close friends, but I liked the guy. He was kind of a wise guy," said Dan as he smiled at the memory. "But he was smart enough not to wise off to the nuns."

"Did you talk back to the nuns?"

"Never. I was afraid if I did, the nun would call my mother, then there would be hell to pay. That I didn't want."

The mention of Mike's name triggered a memory. Dan recalled the day not long after Champ's funeral when he paid a visit to Sam Patterson, Coltonwood's veterans' agent. Dan hadn't made an appointment, so he caught Patterson unaware. Patterson pretended not to know Dan. With a tentative glance, Patterson spoke. "Can I help you?"

"That depends. I'd like to speak to you about Mike Dello Russo, a local veteran."

"What about him?"

" I want to know why you haven't helped him and other veterans like him. Isn't that what you do?"

"Mr. Dello Russo has never asked for help."

"Haven't you ever heard of outreach? Most people like Mike are not going to ask for help. You need to go to him. To ask him what he needs."

Sam offered a smile that was not pleasant. "Are you going to have your brother, the mayor, fire me? Is that why you're here?"

"I'm here as a friend of Mike's, not as a representative of the mayor."

"I see. But there's little I can do unless Mr. Dello Russo asks for my help. Why don't you suggest he come see me?"

Dan had realized he wasn't going to get anywhere with this guy. Patterson was a local guy also, a disabled veteran who had been appointed by a previous mayor. He knew his job was safe regardless of how little he did. Dan left. He wondered if he should have a reporter interview Patterson, and pepper him with tough questions he couldn't fudge. In the end, Dan did nothing. There was nothing to do. Sam Patterson was an entrenched city employee and nothing short of his retirement would change that.

"Why did you start with the Fourth of July?" asked Rosalina.

"Because things got really interesting when my bad boy cousins, Anthony and Girard, would visit for the Fourth."

Rosalina puckered her brow. "I don't recall ever meeting them."

"Consider yourself lucky."

I love the Fourth of July, at least I used to. Every year on the Fourth of July my cousins from New Jersey, Anthony and Girard, visit. And every year my brother Champ and I are expected to entertain them. My first mistake was taking them to one of the old burying grounds in town to look at the tombstones. One inscription caught our eyes and led to our creation of a game of settlers and Indians. The tombstone read, "Capt. Hutchinson, Killed by Treacherous Indians." Of course, Anthony had to be Capt. Hutchinson since he always had to be first or the leader in whatever we happened to be doing. His brother Girard would do whatever Anthony would tell him. Girard will someday make history since he's the only known human to have been born without a brain.

Our game went on until close to the last day of my cousins' stay when a neighbor told us to get lost, that we had no business playing a game on sacred ground. That should have been the end of our time in the old cemetery except that Anthony spotted an old tomb that was actually built into a hillside. Anthony decided that he needed to see what was inside.

The cousins arrived around noon and Anthony was ready to set his plan in motion. He asked to borrow the keys to his father's car, telling Uncle Hank he needed something in the car. Uncle Hank was well into his second or third beer and gave the keys to his son. Anthony took a tire iron from the car and quickly stuffed it inside his sweatshirt. This may not seem odd except that no one in his right mind would be wearing a sweatshirt in ninety-five-degree heat. The plan was to take the tire iron to the old cemetery and stash it there until that night when we would sneak into the cemetery and break into the tomb.

We had to take a detour so as few people as possible would see us. We couldn't cut through any yards as we would do at night, so we had to pretend we were going to my school to look around. This was what I told Mum as we were leaving. I hate lying to my mother and resolved never to do it again. Confession next Saturday for sure.

We ducked and dodged our way to the cemetery where Anthony hid the tire iron amid a tangle of weeds growing beside the tomb. The weeds were as tall as we were and covered in burrs that stuck to your clothes. The rest of the day was torture, knowing that we were going to be doing something that was not only wrong but probably illegal as well.

Along with being old and dark, the cemetery has a giant tree to the left of the entrance that has two enormous limbs that stretch out and up like two giant arms. It has a name: The Great Spirit Tree, and people say that the tree is guarding the graveyard and will grab and kill anyone seen in the cemetery after dark. I kept looking at the tree as we crept into the cemetery. I was hoping someone would see us and stop us. I could hear traffic downtown and wanted to be home reading a good book.

When we reached the tomb, Anthony found the tire iron and slid it under the rusted wire that covered a window of the tomb. He pushed and pulled but the old wire held and left only a fine dust on his clothes and hands. Suddenly, we heard glass breaking. The tire iron's curved end slipped out of his hand and broke the glass behind the wire. The next thing I knew Anthony was rolling on the ground, pulling at his hair, and screaming.

"A bat. There's a bat in my hair," he yelled as he clawed the back of his head.

Girard, who had tried to help Anthony, was suddenly hopping around, and screaming, "My finger! It bit my finger."

There was no way I was going to touch a bat, but I offered a Kleenex to Girard to put around his bloody finger. Champ, who had not said a word during all of this, found his voice. "I'll go get Dad."

Anthony lay on the ground kicking and rolling around. His body crushed the big weed beside the tomb and his legs kicked pieces of weed into the air. I hunched down to get a better look and I could see the bat's head. The poor creature was terrified and exhausted as it tried to free itself from Anthony's hair.

As I expected, someone heard Anthony yelling and called the police. Headlights gradually got brighter as the cruiser inched its way along the dirt road. Girard waved the policeman to where Anthony rolled and kicked on the ground.

"What's the matter here?" asked a cop I knew by sight.

Girard said nothing so I explained, "My cousin has a bat in his hair."

"How the hell did that happen?"

Without waiting for an answer, the cop took a jackknife from his belt and grabbed Anthony's hair, none too gently.

"Ouch. Don't pull my hair," whined Anthony.

"Shut up, you big baby. I have to grab your hair to get this thing free. Consider this a free haircut."

Snip, snip, and the bat disappeared into the night.

The cop helped Anthony to his feet just as Dad and Uncle Hank drove up. They made their way slowly to the tomb, Uncle Hank almost falling. I could hear him curse.

"Hi, Bert," was the cop's greeting to Dad. "Are these guys yours?"

"One of them is. The other two are my nephews."

"Someone heard screaming from the cemetery and called in. I found this boy on the ground with a bat in his hair. I managed to cut it free with my knife. No idea what they're doing here."

Dad turned to me. "Chip, what are you doing here?"

I knew enough not to lie, so I said, "We tried to break into the old tomb. Anthony wanted to see what was inside." As I spoke, I realized Champ was nowhere to be found.

No sooner had I said this than Uncle Hank slapped Anthony so hard he slammed to the ground and looked up in terror. I never thought I would ever feel sorry for Anthony for any reason, but I did just then. The cop helped Anthony to his feet and said to Uncle Hank, "That really wasn't necessary, sir."

Uncle Hank turned on the cop. "He's my kid and I'll hit him if I want to hit him. No business of yours."

"Assault is my business, sir. I can run you in for that, especially when a minor is involved. And there is still the matter of the damage to the tomb. You're liable for that."

Uncle Hank cursed again and moved toward the cop. Dad stepped in front of him.

"Easy, Hank." To the cop he said, "I'll cover whatever damage was done to the tomb. My sons were here too. They'll pay me back by working extra hours in the store. I want them to take responsibility for what they've done."

The cop looked at Anthony and said, "This boy is going to need a rabies shot. I can take him to the hospital in the squad car. Anyone else bitten?"

Girard held up his hand. "I was bit."

"Ok. You go to the hospital too. A rabies shot is very painful. I hope you guys have learned a lesson from this." Anthony and Girard said nothing. I kicked some pieces of weed under my shoes. At that moment I could have easily killed both of my cousins with my bare hands. I will pay Johnny M., the town bully, to beat up both of them next year when they come to visit.

I looked at the Great Spirit Tree as it waved its enormous branches against the night sky.

When I got home, Mum was waiting in the kitchen. "Get up to bed, young man" was all she said.

I woke up the next morning to the sound of the birds singing. Usually, Mum cooks a big breakfast on the Fourth, but not this year. My hands were filthy from last night and I had burrs stuck in my hair. A quick shower cleaned me up but didn't help my mood. Downstairs, I found Mum ironing in the dining room. She said, "Get your own breakfast."

'All right.' She hasn't been this mad since Champ swung a golf club in the house and broke her St. Anthony statue, her favorite. I poured some cereal into a bowl but ate very little. As I was cleaning up the dishes, the doorbell rang. It was Grammy.

"I'm looking for someone to go for a walk with me," she said.

A walk? That's something old people do. "Only Mum's around," I told Grammy. "And she's busy ironing."

"Then you come with me."

"Ok."

We walked in the direction of Main St. where people were setting up chairs already for the parade. I saw the old cemetery out of the corner of my eye, and quickly looked away.

Grammy got right to the point. "What happened last night?" I told her the story since I remembered every detail, every sound, every word spoken.

Grammy spoke again. "I hope you realize that what you did was not very nice. Have you learned from this?"

"Yes. I learned that I really hate Anthony. He's such a jerk."

"Don't talk that way about your cousin. He's not that bad. That's not what I hoped you learned. Anything else?"

I thought a minute. "I learned to think twice before I let someone talk me into doing something I know isn't right. Next time I see Anthony I'm going to tell him to stay away from me. He's such a jerk. Did you know that Uncle Hank hit Anthony? Is Uncle Hank mean? Dad has never hit any of us, no matter what we did."

"No. Uncle Hank isn't mean. He was just reacting to a situation he didn't expect. Your father has raised more children than Hank has, and he has learned to hold back. Uncle Hank just has a shorter fuse, that's all."

"Maybe, but I'm glad he's not my father."

Grammy looked down at me, her face more serious than usual. "Chip, hold on to what is good. Let go of what's bad."

"What does that mean?

"It means that you have a good family, a good neighborhood, good friends, you go to a good school, and you're a good boy, at least most of the time. A lot of people are not as lucky as you are. Avoid trouble whenever you can, walk away if you have to. You can't avoid all that's bad in this world, but you can decide how you will deal with it when it comes your way. What you did last night was a mistake. Make sure you never repeat it. Think about how you feel today. Your parents are mad at you, and your holiday is spoiled. And remember, this is not all Anthony's fault. You and Champ were there, after all. Learn from this and then let it go. End of sermon."

I walked downtown by myself to watch the parade. I found a spot near the end of the route where I could sit on the curb and just watch. As the parade went by, I wondered if I should tell the priest in confession that I want to have Johnny M. beat up Anthony. I also called my cousin a jerk. I should probably mention that also. What happened to the good old days when I had to make up sins so I would have something to say when the priest slid open the wooden panel? All the while, I looked around for Anthony and Girard, but they were nowhere to be found. The parade was as usual with the screaming fire trucks, the bands, floats. All was well until the church float passed in front of me and I realized Sheridan, the idiot altar boy, was riding the float. When he saw me, he started yelling my name and waving like a fool.

"Dan, Dan," he screamed. I looked for a manhole into which I could disappear but found none. I gave him a short wave and caught the Tootsie Roll he threw.

Suddenly I realized the parade was boring and it was time to go home. The sidewalks were still packed with people, and I walked around them as I passed the Common, the fire station, the stores, and all the other businesses on Main St. Then I saw Johnny M. headed straight for me on his bike. He was smiling as though to say, "I got you at last." Feeling doomed, I waded into the crowd and stood next to a lady I didn't even know and acted as if she was my mother. I glanced over my shoulder and saw no sign of Johnny. My route home was now through the woods behind the stores and into backyards, over fences until I reached my street.

Instead of going home, I went to Grammy's. We would be having the cookout there and I thought I might find something to do until everyone else came. The back door was unlocked, which I found strange until I saw Grampy at the table making hamburger patties. He turned quickly at the sound of the door but smiled when he saw me.

"Back already? Is the parade over?"

"No. I just got tired of it, so I decided to leave. Got anything I can do?"

Grampy handed me some potatoes, told me to wash and dry them and wrap them in foil. After I finished that, I was to put them on the grill. As I worked, I realized that I missed Uncle Hank's car in the driveway. I went to the living room to look out at the driveway.

Only Grampy's car was there.

"Um, Grampy, are Aunt Sue and Uncle Hank still here?"

Grampy looked surprised at the question. "No, they left early this morning. They wanted to get a head start on their vacation."

Anthony and Girard were gone. Yes! Now I could enjoy this cookout. I went outside and I could hear the parade in the distance. A band was playing "My Country Tis of Thee" and I sat back on a chaise lounge, eyes closed, as happy as I always used to be on the Fourth of July.

Chapter 2

Aside from his own amusement, Dan found the journal to be a boon in another way. He could read it to his mother during his visits to her in the nursing home. Mrs. Kerr had become non-verbal and unable to converse. She would occasionally speak, but whatever she said was incomprehensible. At least the journal would fill in the long intervals of silence.

Dan had reread the first two entries before the idea to read to his mother had occurred to him. Now was the time to see if the journal could elicit any response from Mrs. Kerr. After his customary kiss on his mother's cheek, Dan settled himself in an uncomfortable chair and began to read.

Mrs. Kerr looked on impassively as Dan read one entry. Her response was no response. Dejected, Dan kissed his mother and departed.

Instead of going home, Dan decided to visit his father who still lived in the family home with Bridy.

"Hi, Dad. How are you feeling these days?"

"I'm all right. Nothing's the same, but I'm all right."

"Are you eating enough?"

"Bridy's a good cook for a single girl. I really don't have much of an appetite these days."

After a tiny pause, Dan said, "I just went to see Mum, and I read to her from my journal. I was really hoping that she would have some kind of reaction, but she didn't. She was sleeping in the chair when I left. It's so hard, you know?"

Mr. Kerr took a deep breath and sighed. "It just doesn't seem fair, after all we went through with Champ. All my life I've believed the everything happens for a reason, but damned if I know why Champ had to be MIA for ten years. He was no sooner found than your mother's illness became the next big problem. It's not fair."

Dan's mind flashed back to the early stages of Mrs. Kerr's illness and how vehemently his father had ignored her symptoms and denied what was crystal clear to everyone else.

"You know, Chip," his father continued. "I really didn't believe that your mother was all that sick. I guess I just didn't want to believe it. Now she doesn't even know who I am. When I got the cancer diagnosis, I was sure that I would die first. Now here I am doing just fine, and your mother is the one who died yet she still lives. I just don't get it."

Dan wanted to comfort his father, but he didn't know how. "I know, Dad, I know. Where's Bridy?"

"She went to Boston for the day. I wish she would meet someone and get married. This is no life for her living with me. She's a fine girl and a smart girl. I don't know why she's still single."

"Not everyone gets married young, Dad. I didn't meet Rosalina until I was almost thirty. Bridy still has her whole life in front of her. Who knows where she'll be a year from now."

Mr. Kerr's smile was wistful. "I do enjoy having her here. This house never seemed so big before. Sometimes I hated all the noise, now I hate the silence even more."

"Have you ever thought of moving, Dad, maybe to an apartment or even a smaller house?"

"No. I want to die here. This is my home; my fondest memories are here. I like familiarity. Besides, where would I find neighbors like the Salinas? Francesca is one of a kind and Salina gives me free wine. You can't beat that."

As he drove home, Dan wondered how often his siblings visited either parent. He would make it his business to find out. To that end, Dan made his way to city hall to seek out the mayor.

As he ascended the marble staircase, Dan remembered the early days of his courtship with Rosalina who was the previous mayor's secretary. His mind then segued to his early friendship with John Murphy with whom he ran the food pantry. Those days seemed so far off, yet all had occurred less than a decade ago.

Dan didn't know the current mayor's secretary who gave him a less than friendly glance as he entered the office.

"Yes? Do you have some business with the mayor?"

Dan flashed what he thought was his most charming smile. "I don't have an appointment. I'm the mayor's brother."

The secretary was unimpressed. "The mayor will not see anyone who doesn't have an appointment."

Fed up with the secretary's imperious attitude, Dan said, "He'll see me. Not only am I his brother, but I'm also the managing editor of the Clarion, the paper that pretty much ruined the administration and reputation of the mayor's predecessor. We sometimes even take aim at city employees, especially those with bad attitudes."

The secretary gaped at Dan who strolled to the massive door of the mayor's office and tapped lightly.

Dan slowly turned the handle but stopped dead in his tracks when he saw his brother tilted back in his chair with a disheveled young woman in his lap, sharing a joint. The mayor whirled but was rendered speechless by the sight of his brother at the door. Once Dan recovered from the shock, he addressed his brother. "You should lock the door when you're having a private party." Dan slammed the door and stalked out in disgust.

When he reached his car, Dan fumbled with the keys, his mind fuddled by the shock of what he had just seen. He couldn't fathom how his brother could so casually engage in scandalous conduct, in his office no less. Dan could hardly comprehend that the older brother whom he had idolized had sunk to such depravity. Hardly aware of what he was doing, Dan drove to a coffee shop and ordered a latte which he sipped moodily as he tried to calm his agitated mind. What else had his brother done? What if this incident became public? The Kerr family would be disgraced. As the managing editor of the paper, Dan could squelch any spurious stories about the mayor, but he could not stop malicious gossip or innuendo. Dan was furious that his brother had so thoughtlessly flaunted the trust of the people who had voted him into office. And what of his family? The mayor was a married man with children. What of his parents and siblings? Public opinion would paint the whole family with the same brush of disgrace. Dan wished he had never set foot in city hall.

Dan had to tell Rosalina, but he would have to wait until they were alone. He wasn't about to broach such a sensitive subject in front of Marla. Since he had to remain quiet, dinner was an ordeal for Dan. He had to act as though everything was normal; to speak of ordinary things, but inside he was seething. Rosalina suspected trouble, but she too remained silent in front of her daughter.

Usually, Marla would eat dinner quietly in her habitual self-absorption. Tonight was different. She prattled on endlessly about the cutest boy in her class whom she was sure wanted to ask her out. As much as he liked Marla, Dan was tempted to lunge across the table and strangle her.

"Don't you have any homework tonight?" Dan finally asked.

"No sweat," replied Marla." I did it all in study hall. My classes are all a joke anyway. All my teachers are dorks. I could pass all my classes even if I did nothing."

This last remark brought a sharp rebuke from her mother. "I'll be going to see all these teachers soon. Then we'll see who the dork is. You just remember that."

After a histrionic eye roll, Marla had an epiphany: she did have some math homework to do. Once Marla was out of earshot, Rosalina accosted Dan. "What's wrong? Is it your mother?"

"No. My brother."

"Pup? What do you mean?"

Dan faced Rosalina. "I stopped by his office today and when I opened the door, I saw a young woman in his lap. They were sharing a joint."

Rosalina gasped and put a hand over her mouth. She asked tentatively, "Was the young woman clothed?"

"She was. I didn't see any more because I slammed the door in disgust and left. Pup's secretary is a winner. Do you know her? I wonder if she knows what's going on."

Rosalina smiled. "I do know her. In fact, she thought she was going to get my job with the previous administration. When I was appointed, she stopped speaking to me."

"Really? I told her the paper sometimes does stories about incompetent city employees. I think that scared her."

Fingering her coffee cup, Rosalina said, "She's very loyal to her boss, whoever that might be. It's likely she does know what's going on, but loyalty keeps her quiet."

Dan felt better once he had shared what he had seen. "Well, the hell with her. What am I going to do about Pup? I want to confront him, but he thrives on confrontation. He's the master at turning around any bad situation he's in and blaming someone else."

"I know this is a delicate and difficult situation," said Rosalina, looking pensive, "but you can't just sweep it under the rug. Sooner or later his conduct will become public knowledge. That will create a huge problem for you as the managing editor of the paper. Something has to be done before people start talking, and you know they will."

Dan's glance at Rosalina was bleak. "Have you heard any gossip about him?"

"No, I haven't. But the school department has enough of its own drama to keep people buzzing. I presume the young woman works at city hall?"

"Probably, but I don't have a clue who she is. I can't very well start asking questions without arousing suspicion."

Rosalina smiled. "I'll keep my ear to the ground. Most secretaries are notorious gossips. I'll pay more attention now that I know this."

Dan still did not have a plan a week after the incident involving his brother. Pup never called. It was as though nothing had ever happened. A couple of times Dan picked up the phone to call Pup, but he hesitated each time. What could he say? The more time that went by, the more Dan conceded the advantage to Pup. Dan almost forgot why he needed to see his brother when he went to city hall that day. Every time he thought about what he had seen, Dan became more incensed at himself for being too craven to confront his brother. What was he afraid of? Until Dan could answer that question, he would not be able to mention the incident to his volatile sibling.

Dan's consternation about confronting Pup ended abruptly when Pup called him.

"Hey, Chip. You know that the old man is going to be eighty-five next month, and Mimi and I decided he should have a party."

Irked, Dan replied, "Since when do you and Mimi decide for everyone else? Does Dad even want a party? I'll bet he doesn't."

"Well, he says he doesn't, but Mimi thinks that even though he says he doesn't, he really does so we should have the party."

"Let me get this straight. Dad doesn't want a party, but we should give him one anyway because he really does want one. That's pretty convoluted logic don't you think? It makes no sense to me."

"No matter. Could you tell Gabby, Bridy, and Biddy? Mimi already told Cissy."

"Sounds like a done deal to me."

"Come on, the old man will love it. He doesn't have much to be happy about with Mum in the nursing home."

"Is this a surprise?"

"Yeah, it is. Elaine and I are going to host."

"Fine."

"What are you so touchy about?"

When Dan didn't reply, Pup said, "You know that thing you saw a few weeks ago? It was nothing."

"Are you kidding me? It was nothing? What if a city councilor or even a taxpayer had seen that? Then what?"

"The councilors are all on the take anyway. I have more dirt on them than they'll ever have on me."

"That's not the point, Pup. You're the mayor, an elected official. Why do you think you can smoke dope in your office with a young woman on your lap? Do you really think that people would just overlook that? The hell they would."

"Nobody cares so let's just pretend you never saw it."

"Just like that? Pretend I never saw a thing? What's wrong with you?"

"Well, are you on board for the party or not?"

The abrupt change in conversation shook Dan for a moment.

"I'll get back to you on that."

Dan's concern about his brother reached another level after this conversation. Pup's cavalier attitude about such a serious breach of protocol alarmed Dan. Then another thought unnerved him even more. What if the young woman talked? She had probably told people at city hall already. It was just a matter of time until the whole debacle blew up in Pup's face. Dan knew that Pup would make the affair even more sordid by lying about it. No doubt Pup would throw the young woman under the bus to save his own skin.

Tired in every fiber of his being, Dan reclined in his chair, his feet on the desk. He needed to find a way to deal with this nightmare, to save his own sanity if nothing else. Then it hit him. He and Rosalina would take a vacation. They hadn't been away since their honeymoon. What better time to pack their bags and escape their troubles?

Dan wanted to surprise Rosalina, so he made all the arrangements and requested vacation time before he broke the news. Rosalina was delighted at the prospect of a cruise to St. Maarten. They would leave in two weeks, then Dan would be free of Pup and the plans for this ridiculous party. He desperately hoped that nothing major would happen that would force him to cancel the trip.

Chapter 3

Dan decided to take his journal along on the trip. He hadn't opened it since his futile attempt to engage his mother in conversation. Now maybe he could find some solace in looking back to a time when the family was united and happy.

Dan took his journal to the solarium to read. He had no sooner settled himself than the steward brought him a beer unbidden.

"Thank you, Marcel. Do you always remember the passengers' favorite labels?"

"Yes, sir. I do my best to remember peoples' preferences."

"I'm impressed."

"Thank you, sir. Will madame be joining you soon? If so, I will bring her a glass of Pinot Noir."

"She's getting a massage right now. She may afterwards."

"Very good, sir. I will check again later."

The beer tasted great as Dan read the chapter about his twelfth birthday. He did remember most of the details. Why had he even brought a diary he had written when he was eleven on a cruise with his wife? To forget and to remember.

Today is my twelfth birthday. All day at school I was thinking about my party that was to be during supper. In my family, everyone gets to have their favorite meal on their birthday so we're having lamb chops tonight. All my family is here for dinner. Gram and Gramp gave me a typewriter since I want to be a writer. I never expected such a gift. Grammy and Grampy gave me a new suit including a shirt and tie. Didn't expect that either. Mimi and Neil gave me movie tickets. I like this since the Stooges are supposed to release a full-length movie later this year. Mum and Dad gave me a new bike. Again, I didn't expect this at all. My sibs all chipped in to buy me a Cross pen set.

The Salinas came over for cake and coffee and Mrs. Salina surprised me again when she gave me an Etch A Sketch which I've been wanting forever. The present was from the entire Salina family, and I imagined Angelina actually deciding on the gift and buying it herself. It probably didn't happen that way, but I can dream.

This was the best birthday I've ever had.

Dan was well aware the past was gone forever, never to be recaptured. He also knew that time had its way with everything. Dan wanted to forget his mother's illness, Pup's erratic behavior, and the agonizing wait for Champ's remains to be found. He wanted the family to be as it had been in his childhood, free from the animosities that had developed over the years. Since there was no way to reel time back, Dan had to be content to find solace in memories, as ephemeral as they might be.

Rosalina found Dan asleep in his chair, the diary splayed across his chest. He awoke when she picked it up. He saw her curiously examining the dog-eared notebook.

"Why did you take this on a cruise? I thought you already read this from cover to cover."

Dan, embarrassed, said, " I like to read it. It's comforting and so different from the present."

Hoping to divert Rosalina, Dan said, "Marcel was wondering if you wanted a glass of wine. He said he'd be back."

As if on cue, Marcel appeared with a flute of Pinot for Rosalina, who stretched out on the lounge chair and took a deep, satisfying swallow of her wine. She turned to her husband.

"You can't repeat the past. It's over and done with."

"I'm not trying to repeat the past. I like to read the diary for the same reason that people look at old photo albums, to remember the good times. It makes me sad to see how fractured the family has become. But at least you and I are happy."

Rosalina reached for Dan's hand. "I don't mean to criticize. It's just that I worry sometimes that you get too caught up with the past. Is it healthy to dwell on what's gone by? Things won't always be the way they are now. Everything changes. Bad times don't last."

Dan knew that his wife spoke the truth, but he couldn't just fling the diary in the trash and pretend that it didn't exist. Sometimes he wished his mother had never found it. He should have gotten rid of it years ago. But he didn't. Now the diary was becoming a bone of contention with Rosalina. If he wanted to continue to read it, he would have to do so when Rosalina wasn't around. She had no patience with his wistful sentimentality. He even wondered if she would throw the diary overboard. Busy as they were on the cruise, there was still a lot of down time to fill, and Dan desperately wanted to lose himself in the journal. He saw no harm in indulging in nostalgia.

Dan decided to pack the diary away in the bottom of his suitcase for the rest of the cruise. He knew Rosalina was almost daring him to read it so she could snatch it away. Yet despite its physical absence, Dan found himself thinking of the diary almost obsessively. But since he and Rosalina were together constantly, there was no opportunity to sit and read it. On nights when Rosalina fell asleep first, Dan thought about reading, but he was afraid the light would wake her up. Best not to take that chance.

Even when they were at dinner where he met and enjoyed people from every walk of life and every background, thoughts of the diary lurked at the back of his mind, closely akin to the way memories of Champ would disturb his peace of mind.

As the cruise sailed toward its end point, a vigorous thunderstorm broke out in the dwindling twilight. It was spectacular. Vivid lightning and deafening thunder rocked the massive ship. Dan watched, captivated, from his cabin. The power and majesty of the storm cleared his mind, something that even the gourmet food and choice wines had not been able to do. When the storm finally abated, Dan felt cleansed.

It was not until he was on the plane headed home that Dan found a way to read the diary without Rosalina's knowledge. He would keep it at the office to be read whenever he had a few minutes. When they got home, Dan would simply put the diary into his briefcase. Rosalina would never know.

An exhausted Dan and Rosalina arrived home around noon. Both were short with each other, and they still had to unpack, do laundry and shop for food. The phone rang as Dan was starting a pot of coffee.

"Hello."

"AAAYYY. How was your trip?"

"Hi, Mrs. Salina. It was great, but now we're both tired and hungry. The trip seems like it was a few days ago rather than a few hours."

"That's why I called. Come to dinner tonight. I made lasagna and Salina made a new batch of wine. Five-thirty. Bye."

"Who called?" asked Rosalina as she strolled into the room.

"Francesca. We're invited to dinner tonight at five-thirty."

"Fantastic. Now I don't have to worry about cooking. I've never been so tired after a vacation before. Must be getting old."

Dan and Rosalina cuddled together on the couch. As each one started to drift off, despite the coffee, Marla and her suitcase came barging through the front door. Petulant and testy, she flung her bag onto a chair and flounced into the kitchen without a word of greeting to Dan or Rosalina.

Confused, a sleepy Rosalina called, "Why are you home so early? I thought you were staying with your grandparents until tonight."

"I told them to take me home early. I couldn't stand being there another minute."

"Why? What happened?"

"Nothing happened. They smothered me the whole week. I couldn't do anything without their permission. They treated me like I was a five-year-old."

"Just remember you were in their home and subject to their rules. Some day you will know what a difficult responsibility it is to care for someone else's child."

"I'm not a child. I'm a senior in high school."

Rosalina was too weary to argue with her daughter. When she said nothing, Marla asked sarcastically, "How was the cruise?"

"The cruise was wonderful, but we're both tired from traveling."

"Why couldn't I go with you?"

"I was not about to pull you out of school for a week to go on a cruise."

"You just wanted to be alone so you and Dan could have some nooky-nooky."

"Don't you talk like that in this house. You shouldn't wonder why your grandparents were so strict with you. Your attitude is really irking me."

"It would not make any difference if I missed school for a week. I could be out for a month and not miss a thing. My classes are a joke. My only decent teacher had a baby and left. All the rest are absolute dorks. I can't wait to go to college."

"Neither can I."

When the hostilities between Rosalina and Marla finally subsided, Marla agreed reluctantly to have dinner with the Salinas. The three of them walked to their neighbors' house. No sooner had they crossed the threshold, than Salina handed Rosalina and Dan glasses of wine. Sulky Marla had to be content with Pepsi. When they entered the dining room, they received a smart shock. Mr. Kerr and Bridy were sitting at the table.

Dan was somewhat alarmed at how his father looked. He and Rosalina had only been gone for a week, but Mr. Kerr seemed to have aged a couple of years.

"Hi, Dad. How's Mum?"

"She's the same, no change."

"Does she talk at all?"

"No. She never talks anymore."

Bridy interjected, "You both look tanned and relaxed. The cruise did you good."

Rosalina responded, "It was wonderful. We will definitely be going on another one. I've never been so relaxed or pampered."

As Bridy and Rosalina exchanged pleasantries, Dan watched his father closely.

His hair seemed whiter, his face more seamed. All the anxiety and worry that Dan had managed to forget, came flooding back. Francesca put an arm around Dan's waist. "You ready to eat?"

"More than ready," exclaimed Dan.

The meal was rich and satisfying. As good as the food on the cruise had been, no one else could cook like Francesca. Dan felt deeply grateful that he and Rosalina could enjoy this intimate dinner with old friends. It was certainly better than being home listening to Rosalina and Marla argue.

Francesca kept everyone laughing with anecdotes of her trip from Italy to the United States. "The boat, it rock the whole time. I was ready to jump over the side. I hate boats ever since. No cruises for me."

Somehow while Francesca was entertaining, Marla had slipped herself some wine. With each sip she became redder in the face and looser in the tongue.

"Mrs. Salina," Marla lisped. "I smoke pot at least once a week. You should try it. It's better than a cruise."

Dead silence at the table. Rosalina, horrified, nearly choked on a piece of Italian bread. Everyone stared at Marla who chatted on obliviously.

"The cutest boy in my class wants to go out with me. I'm what the boys call a Wendy, hot and juicy. But I'm going to the prom with a guy who's as hot as they come and…"

Marla never finished the sentence as her mother slapped her smartly across the face.

"You are never to speak like this ever again in front of anyone. You owe everyone at this table an apology, especially Mr. and Mrs. Salina and your grandfather. I've never been more ashamed. I'm disgusted with your attitude and your mouth. You should be ashamed of yourself."

A chastised Marla ducked her head and muttered, "I'm sorry. I don't usually talk this way. It's the wine."

Francesca screamed at her husband, "Why you let her have wine? Stunada. She's not old enough to drink. Now you see what you did."

The aggrieved party countered, "I was drinking wine when I was eleven or twelve. Kids drink wine in Italy. You forget that your daughters drank wine before they were old enough. What's your problem now?"

"This girl is a guest, not one of our own. Her mother should decide if she can have wine or not."

Marla stood so suddenly that her chair banged to the floor. "Everyone just shut up. I drank the wine because I wanted to. Nobody made me. I'm going home."

The slightly tipsy teen stomped out of the house.

Rosalina was furious. "I'll kill her when I get home. I'm so sorry that my daughter made such a fool of herself. My apologies to all of you. She used to be such a good child. I don't know who she is anymore."

"AAAYYY. My three girls make yours look tame. I raised three stunadas. Everyone ready for coffee?"

Dan, anticipating the fireworks when they went home, groaned, "Back to reality."

Luckily for Dan, his ever-efficient secretary, Rachel, pulled double duty during his vacation. Yet, there was much Dan had to attend to himself upon his return to work. He was pretty much back into the old routine when Rachel buzzed. "Mayor Kerr is on line 2."

"Hello, Pup. I'm really busy."

"This won't take long. I want to tell you that Dad's party is going to be a '40s theme party. Mimi knows of some guy in Huston who plays the organ and specializes in songs from the 40s. Dad will love it. And don't forget your bathing suit."

"Wait a minute. The party is a birthday/ pool/ 40s theme party? Why don't you hire a dancing horse or sword swallower? This party is getting totally out of control."

"No way. How many times will Dad be eighty-five?"

"Don't you ever work? You seem to spend all your time planning parties."

"Hey, I can take some time away from my official duties. I'm a family guy, after all."

"I'm happy for you, but I do work, and I'd like to get back to it. Is that it?"

"Yup. Go back to work. I have to attend the VFW luncheon. Bye."

After Dan hung up, it occurred to him that Pup hadn't even asked how the cruise had been. No real surprise considering it was his totally self-absorbed brother.

Dan's phone rang again. It was Henry, one of the editors.

"Hey, Dan. A guy who wouldn't give his name called and said that the mayor is playing fast and loose with some chicks at city hall."

Dan sat up straight in his chair. "The mayor?"

Yeah. No sources or names. It's probably just a nasty rumor."

"I hope it is. Well, we don't publish rumors. Let me know if you hear anything else."

"Will do."

Dan sank his head into his hands. "Oh, God. Someone squealed."

Chapter 4

Once Dan recovered his equilibrium, he immediately called Bridy, who, fortunately, answered the phone.

"Bridy, I need to talk to you right now. Just say yes or no. Don't give Dad any indication of what you're talking about."

"Yes."

"We need to meet at my house right now. Give Dad some phony story that you forgot something at the store, or whatever. I'll meet you there in fifteen minutes."

Bridy assumed it was something to do with the birthday party. She left the house, telling her father that she was going to the library. She drove to Dan's home and made sure she parked the car out of sight behind some bushes.

As she waited for Dan, she wondered what could possibly be so urgent. The party was Pup's idea and responsibility. Why was Dan so riled up?

Dan pulled in and they made for the house. He wasted no time informing Bridy why he needed to see her so urgently. "I have something to share with you and it involves Pup. About a month ago, I went to city hall to see him about something or other, and I saw him with a young woman in his lap and they were sharing a joint."

Bridy gasped. "At his office?"

"Yes. Later when I tried to talk to him about this, he fluffed it off. Anyway, today the paper got an anonymous call from some guy who said that the mayor was playing fast and loose with some chicks at city hall or words to that effect."

"So, people suspect that his conduct is less than stellar."

"Yes. If this becomes public knowledge, he will probably be recalled from office. Think of the effect that will have on Dad. The family will be disgraced."

"You need to talk to him post haste. Pup has always been full of himself, but I didn't think he would go to such an extreme. He wouldn't pay any attention to me since he thinks I'm still ten years old."

"I'd love to have a reporter check into this, but that would only arouse more suspicion. Rosie has been paying attention to what she hears at work, but so far no one has been gossiping about Pup. But you're right. I will have to confront him. I can't believe he would be so brazen and so stupid."

"You have to do something, and soon."

With sudden resolve, Dan said, "I'll pay him a visit right now." Dan hugged and thanked his younger sister and made his way to see the mayor.

Dan stormed into the lavish office at city hall. He ignored the dragon lady who demanded, "What do you think you're doing? You can't just walk into the mayor's office without an appointment."

Undeterred, Dan flung open the oak door to the inner sanctum where His Honor sat alone at his desk.

The mayor looked up. "What the hell? What do you mean by barging in here?"

"I'll tell you what I mean. I want to know if it's true that you're having flings with women who work here."

"Isn't that my business?"

"As a citizen and a taxpayer, it's my business. Is it true, or isn't it?"

"Why do you care? Where did you hear this?"

"Someone called the paper and said that you were fooling around with women who work at city hall."

His Honor gave his brother a snarky smile. "You believe what an anonymous caller said about me? Is that how your paper operates? Pretty sad, if you ask me."

"Don't forget, Pup, that I saw you with a young woman in your lap in your office during working hours. Don't pull that choir boy act with me. I know you too well."

"What's there to discuss if you know me that well? Would you like me to arrange something for you? Most of the women here are more than willing."

Dan's temper finally cracked. "Dammit, Pup," he yelled and slammed his fists on the desk. "Can't you see that what you're doing is wrong? It demeans you and the office you hold. What's wrong with you? Why can't you understand this?"

The mayor sat back in his chair. "Take it easy, bro. You're overreacting. You make it sound like I'm running an escort service out of the office. I'm in control here. There won't be any scandals during my administration if that's what you're worried about."

Dan ran his hands through his hair, incredulous at his brother's stubbornness. "Pup, will you wake up in life? All it takes is one accusation, just one, and you're finished. Then what? You're no longer mayor and the family is disgraced. Is that what you want? Don't think it can't happen, because it most certainly can."

The mayor laughed. "My approval rating is above eighty percent. The people don't care what I do as long as I lower taxes and show up at every goddamned event in this city. They love me. I'm a character, like some of those old-time pols. When times are good, people aren't concerned about what the mayor does privately. Besides, if someone does accuse me of something, I'll deny it to the hilt, and it will blow over. No big deal. The people of this city are in my hip pocket. My second term is just about guaranteed."

"What kind of fantasy world do you inhabit, Pup? You think you can do and say anything, and the voters will forgive you because you're such a card and a throwback to the old days of flamboyant politicians? WILL YOU GET REAL? WILL YOUR BALLOON EVER LAND? If someone does come out and accuse you of scandalous conduct, the voters will toss your naive ass into the street quicker than you can say, '"I like Ike."'

"Ha, ha. You're a riot, Chip. Now you sound like Aunt Julia. Did you switch to her brand of whiskey?"

"Ok. I give up. Do as you please and ruin your reputation and disgrace the family. You're sitting on a powder keg, and you don't even know it. You are a friggin' idiot."

The door opened and the dragon lady poked her head into the office. "Would you like me to call the police, Mr. Mayor?"

Dan rounded on her. "Get out! This does not concern you."

The mayor held up his palms to her. "It's ok, Lillian. My brother and I are discussing family matters, and he tends to get carried away. There's no problem."

Dan sputtered, "Family matters? As if you care about family matters or anything else for that matter. Go to hell."

The mayor's surprise lasted only a moment. "Don't forget the party is at noon on Saturday. Don't be late."

The door slammed.

After the argument with Pup, Dan went back to work, but he couldn't concentrate. As hard as he tried, he couldn't rid his mind of one nagging thought; if the mayor didn't happen to be his brother, would he have warned him? Likely not since every reporter, especially ones who worked for a small paper, would salivate at such a potentially explosive story. Family should always come first, he kept telling himself, but what would happen if the story did make the headlines? The mere thought of it gave Dan a migraine so he pushed the thought out of his mind, or he tried to.

Chapter 5

Saturday was a big day for the Kerr family. It was the patriarch's eighty-fifth birthday. Since their blowup on Thursday, Dan hadn't spoken to his brother, nor did he want to. Still Dan deeply regretted his behavior and the language he used. He knew he would have to apologize, but his lingering anger precluded it.

Bryant had come home from college for the weekend, so Dan and family went out to eat. Dan was deeply touched that his stepson gave up his weekend to attend a party for an eighty-five-year-old man.

Since the party was a surprise, all the guests were asked to be a half hour early. The party was crowded when Dan and Rosalina, Bryant, and Marla arrived. All of the Kerr siblings, except for Bridy, were there. In addition to the entire Kerr clan, there were many other people milling around. The host, His Honor, was resplendent in blindingly white pants and a magenta shirt with matching sunglasses. Pup greeted Dan and family courteously, saying nothing about the confrontation at city hall.

Bridy arrived with both parents. Mrs. Kerr had been given a five-hour pass to attend the party. All the guests applauded as the guest of honor had a white carnation pinned to his shirt by Mimi and Pup presented his mother with a corsage of cymbidium orchids.

The organist who specialized in 40s tunes began to play as the honored guest and his wife made their way to the table reserved for them. Aunt Julia sat at the next table with her dedicated caregiver, Ramona, by her side. As was her custom, Aunt Julia defied all sartorial decorum by wearing a dress that made her look like a quivering bowl of fruit salad.

Dan surveyed the crowd and saw elected officials mingling with the family. The party, as least as Dan understood, was supposed to be family and close friends only. The more he looked, the more familiar faces he saw, including Hank Goodwin, the chair of the school committee, and Bettina Frawley who worked as the city assessor. Dan's anger boiled again when he realized why Pup wanted to host. It was his chance to turn a family gathering into a political event.

Dan was momentarily distracted by his nephew Matty.

"Uncle Chip," yelled Matty from across the yard. "I won second prize in my school's art fair."

"That's great, Matty. Looks like we'll have a Rembrandt in the family."

"A what?"

"A famous painter."

The boy beamed up at Dan. "Did he win any prizes?"

"Oh, yes, many.

As he spoke to his nephew, Dan spotted Laura Bridgewater making her way around the yard, drink in hand, hugging and kissing everyone as though she owned the place. What the hell was she doing here? She was the reporter who wrote a scathing article about the then new Mayor Kerr. Dan thought that Pup hated her guts. Apparently not. Then it hit Dan. Was Pup having a fling with Laura to gain favorable publicity for his reelection campaign? If this were the case, and Dan could prove it, he would fire Laura on the spot, even if she was the paper's best reporter.

Eventually, Laura sidled up to her boss. "Hi, Dan. I thought you might be here."

"Hi, Laura. Are you working on your day off? Mingling with the very people you usually malign in the paper?"

"The mayor asked me to come," was Laura's clipped reply. "Am I not allowed to socialize with people I interview?"

"It is rather odd, now that you mention it," said Dan. "Be careful of mixing your business and social life. It could get hairy."

Laura, clearly offended, sniffed, "I can handle it." Then she found a city councilor to bait into saying something he shouldn't.

Rosalina knew a lot of the city people at the party, and she was busy talking, so Dan made his way to the table where Aunt Julia held forth. Wait staff in stiff black and white outfits circulated among the guests offering all manner of hors d'oeuvres. Dan grabbed some Swedish meatballs and pulled up a chair next to his favorite aunt who turned her whole body to look at him. "Chippy, I'm so happy to see you. Why don't you visit me more often?"

"I'm very busy at work these days."

"Are you writing a book? I want to read it, but I'm on borrowed time as it is, so make it snappy."

Aunt Julia turned her attention back to her martini and nibbled on a scallop wrapped in bacon. Suddenly her hand clamped down on a chubby fist and dirty fingers. Gabby's son Dylan had tried to grab a scallop off her plate, but Aunt Julia was too quick for him.

"Get your hand off my plate. Grabbing people's food is rude and disgusting. I'm going to speak to your mother and tell her to teach you some manners."

The little miscreant whimpered and writhed to get free, but Aunt Julia was not ready to release him. "How old are you?" bellowed Aunt Julia.

The terrified child only whimpered louder.

"What? What did you say? Speak up. I can't hear you."

With a leer that would frighten an alligator, Aunt Julia lifted her hand and Dylan bolted into the crowd.

Dan said, "Don't you think you were a little hard on him, Aunt Julia? He's only a little kid."

"Not at all," rasped Aunt Julia. "He needs to learn some manners. Grabbing food from other people's plates. The very idea!"

Dan excused himself to Aunt Julia so he could talk to some of the other guests. He was chatting with his brother-in-law, Dexter, when he spotted an older lady on the arm of a young man. Neither was a city employee or a neighbor. Who could they be? As they got closer, Dan recognized his Aunt Sue and his infamous cousin Anthony. Many years had gone by since Dan had seen Anthony, but still he was surprised by how old and shopworn Anthony looked. When they were kids, Dan and Anthony despised each other. Dan had avoided Anthony ever since the incident in the cemetery. Dan considered his cousin a reprobate, a sure career criminal in the making. Yet, Dan was eager to talk to his cousin, despite their past differences.

Anthony recognized Dan immediately and they shook hands. In an attempt to seem casual, Dan asked, "So what are you doing these days, Anthony?"

"Well, for starters, I was in a bad accident about ten years ago which fractured my back and both my legs. I'm on disability since I really can't work. I get migraines so bad I have to stay in a dark room for days. I wish the accident killed me."

Dan, eager to change the subject, said, "What's Girard up to these days?"

"He was smart. He joined the Navy. He's stationed in Florida. I go down a few times a year to visit. I don't have nothin' else to do. I live with my mother, but I can't help her much. I'm pretty much useless."

Despite their history, Dan felt bad for Anthony. Life had dealt him a bad hand, and Anthony being Anthony, had neither the wit nor desire to find a way to make things better.

Dinner was served so Dan found Rosalina and the kids, and they sat down to barbecued steaks, chicken, potato salad, macaroni salad, corn on the cob, and green salad. The hot dogs were for the kids, but Dan grabbed one anyway. It was a satisfying feast, and the beer and wine were plentiful.

The organist continued to play while everyone ate. Dan couldn't believe his eyes when his parents started to dance on the lawn. Even more astounding still was Mrs. Kerr singing along with the music as her children, none of whom she recognized, stared in tearful stunned amazement at their mother. Dan couldn't remember the last time he had heard his mother's voice. Now her sweet soprano lilted over the stunned crowd as she sang, "I'll be with you in apple blossom time. I'll be with you when you change your name to mine." The lady who could not recall the names of her children remembered the words to a song almost half a century old.

The last notes of the song hung in the air and, then as though coming out of a trance, everyone at the party stood and applauded. Mrs. Kerr looked around, a baffled expression on her face. Gently, her husband led her back to her chair. For Dan and his siblings, the world had tilted for just a moment. Dan knew he would remember those few seconds for the rest of his life.

Chapter 6

Conflicting emotions collided in Dan's head the day after the party. He was exhilarated, confused, weary, and depressed. He just wanted to relax on this Sunday morning before he drove Bryant back to college. He and Rosalina and family went out to breakfast and Dan ate as though it would be his last meal. Breakfast was not his favorite, but he feasted on steak and eggs with home fries, bacon, and toast. He tried to wash away his hangover with gallons of coffee. When the family returned home, Dan looked forward to a quiet afternoon with the paper. It was not to be.

Bridy called around eleven o'clock to invite Dan and family to the family home for lunch. Mr. Kerr had been sent home from the party with enough food to feed an army. The last thing Dan wanted was another meal, but he accepted without even asking Rosalina. His wife made no objections, except to remind Dan that they had to return Bryant to school that afternoon.

Mr. Kerr looked flushed and happy following the birthday bash. He bustled around the kitchen as Dan and family seated themselves. He happily poured wine for anyone who wanted some. Dan declined since he had to drive a considerable distance in a few hours.

Marla spoke first. "Grampy, how did you like your party? Were you surprised?"

Mr. Kerr grinned. "I was totally surprised. Bridy did all the planning right under my nose, and I didn't have any idea. That shows how dense I am."

"I had a blast," gushed Marla between bites of cold chicken. "That was the first time I've been out in two weeks." This sally was delivered with a sly glance at her mother. Rosalina had threatened to return Marla's prom dress and cancel her graduation party if Marla didn't behave at her grandfather's party. It had worked. Marla's behavior, though flawless, probably included a few furtive sips of forbidden beverages. Now that her time of being confined to her home was over, Marla was ebullient and talkative. Not so her brother. Bryant was quiet by nature. He lacked the easy, garrulous style of his sister. Bryant's laconic nature used to bother Dan until he came to realize that the boy was just quiet not angry.

Bryant was a junior at UMass, Amherst majoring in business. He wanted to be a stockbroker or a CPA. His temperament suited both occupations perfectly. Bryant had learned a long time ago to just ignore his sister's endless rambling. When Marla paused for breath, Braynt addressed his grandfather. "Grampy, I'll be working for a landscaper for the summer, but I should still be able to mow your lawn, so Dan doesn't have to do it."

"Thank you, Bryant. That's very considerate of you," Mr. Kerr said. "I'm sure Chip appreciates it also."

"I sure do," replied Dan. "I have enough trouble keeping up with my own lawn. Bryant, you'll be tired. Landscaping is long hours in the sun and a lot of hard work, but you're up to the task."

Bryant blushed at the compliment and looked at his plate.

Bridy spoke then. "Did you know that Biddy and Dexter want to start their own business selling cosmetics? I think they're crazy."

"I agree," concurred Mr. Kerr. "Owning your own business means you never get a break from it. You live with it day and night, twenty-four seven. Being your own boss can be good at times, but it also means you have all the headaches."

Dan interjected, "Every job has its good points and bad points. I say let them try. They'll find out soon enough if it's right or wrong for them."

The lunch had to end early to give Dan enough time to get Bryant back to college before early evening. Dan wanted to speak to Bridy privately and to that end he decided he would contact her and arrange a meeting. Bridy was smart and sensible. She wasn't histrionic like Mimi nor anxious and hysterical like Cissy nor insecure and tentative like Gabby. Dan felt he could discuss anything with her and be assured of her cooperation and her silence, if necessary.

Dan met his younger sister a few days later at a Dunkin Donuts in a nearby town. Over coffee and eclairs, Dan told Bridy about his suspicions of Pup and Laura Bridgewater.

"I think they might be having an affair, but, as usual, I don't have any proof. Pup apparently has cozied up her to give himself some good press and to keep his extracurricular activities out of the paper. It's the only reasonable explanation as to why she was at the party."

"But what about the pols who were there at what was supposed to be a family and friends only party?"

"Same thing. Pup wants to keep them in his camp. He needs as many friends as he can find, at least until the election. After that, who knows?"

Bridy looked thoughtful and sad. " I can't believe that Pup would become so corrupt. He always had a huge ego, but this is beyond the pale. I keep thinking of the old saying 'Absolute power corrupts absolutely.'"

"True," agreed Dan. "It makes me wonder what else Pup has done, thinking he can get away with murder. How would that affect Dad?"

"I don't even want to think about that," said Bridy. She continued, "As you know, gossip spreads like wildfire in Coltonwood."

"Chances are good that Dad's McDonald's buddies have heard about Pup and his dalliances. That guy Dick makes it his business to know everything that happens, especially at city hall. We can't protect Dad completely, no matter how discreet we try to be. Let's just play it cool. Pup is likely to hang himself, so just let the chips fall where they may."

Dan and Bridy talked about the birthday party as they finished their coffee and went their separate ways.

Bridy had some business of her own with the mayor that she did not mention to Dan. Since she had time on her hands, the second youngest Kerr decided that she would like to help people who were struggling with caring for a family member with dementia. To set her idea in motion, she had to consult the mayor.

His Honor received his younger sister with a mixture of boredom and fascination. He was well aware of Bridy's success in the retail world that she left to return home and find her niche in some other field. Without a doubt, Bridy had achieved incredible success at a very young age. She was about to begin a second career when most people had just embarked on their first. Even though the mayor tended to treat her with affectionate distance, his younger sister really rather dazzled him. She had style and intelligence, and she was not easily intimidated or discouraged. He would have to be careful how he spoke to her.

"Thanks for taking the time to see me, Pup," Bridy said as she wrapped her oldest brother in a hug. "I won't take too much of your time."

"I always have time for family, you know that. What's on your mind?"

"I'd like to start a support group for families like ours who are dealing with a family member with dementia. When I visit Mum, I talk to people who are in the same boat, so to speak, as we are. They want to talk and share, but the nursing home doesn't provide any forum for that. They need help, and I'd like to help them."

"How does that involve me?"

"Simple. I need a meeting space."

"Won't the nursing home provide that?"

"No, I already asked. If you can find me some space in city hall or some other public building, that would be great."

"The person you need to see is John Murphy. John has been known to work miracles. Look what he did with the food pantry. Go see him and tell him and whatever he recommends, I'll support. As you know, he's Chip's best buddy so he won't brush you off. His office is on the second floor. He should be in."

"Shouldn't I make an appointment first? He might be busy."

"Whatever. Is that it? I have a meeting in ten minutes."

"Thank you, Pup. I really appreciate this."

Bridy went to see John Murphy who was his usual affable self. After some obligatory pleasantries, Bridy got right down to business. "John, I need to find a meeting room for a support group I want to start. I met with the mayor and he told me to see you, so here I am."

"The mayor called me and gave me a brief overview of your project. I think your best bet would be to contact the senior center. There are plenty of meeting rooms that are usually available. If that doesn't work, try the library. Plenty of rooms there too."

"Thank you. I should have thought of the senior center, but it never crossed my mind."

John smiled his amiable grin. "Tell your brother Dan to get his butt in here. I haven't seen him in ages."

"Will do. He always enjoys your chats over coffee."

"How many people do you have in the support group?"

Bridy replied, somewhat sheepishly, " I don't have any yet. I thought I'd find a place to meet before I advertised."

"Ok. When you're ready, let me know and we'll get this show on the road."

Later Bridy tried to recruit her father to join the yet to be formed group. "But, Dad," Bridy remonstrated, "A support group would be good for you. You can talk to people who understand what you're dealing with."

After a long pause, Mr. Kerr replied, "I don't need to discuss my feelings with people I don't know. I've never done that, and I never will."

"You may not know them, but they're in the same boat as you."

"Will that change the situation? Will I feel different after I talk about my feelings? I doubt it."

Bridy, frustrated and exasperated, said, "Of course nothing will change the situation, but you could say how you feel about the situation. Just think about it, ok, Dad?"

"Ok, but don't get your hopes up."

While Bridy was on her personal crusade to begin a dementia support group, Dan was on his own crusade to ascertain if people knew about his brother's hijinks at city hall. As a newspaperman, Dan should have been at the epicenter of news/gossip coming out of city hall, but he felt totally out of the loop. He wondered if people were just being discreet or was there nothing to report. He hoped that the latter was the truth.

It was time for the weekly meeting of the editorial staff. Dan had come to detest these meetings. He sensed some seething animosity under the veneer of professional courtesy. Dan tried his best to be casually pleasant. "Well, gentlemen, what's on the docket for this week?"

Sutcliffe spoke for the group. "We have several potential issues that the paper should take a stand on."

"Such as?"

"The water and sewer rates are due to be hiked again. We stand against that."

"I concur," said Dan. "What else?"

"There's some scuttlebutt about the mayor trying to lure a Hooters to town. We're definitely against that."

Trying to lighten the mood, Dan said, "I would think you yahoos would be interested in Hooters. What's the source?"

"No one. It's just a rumor."

Dan flared, "How many times do I have to tell you guys that this paper does not publish stories based on speculation or hearsay? Either you produce a credible source who's willing to go on the record, or you sidestep the story until you have that source."

Grady, another editor, spoke up. "Newspapers speculate in editorials all the time."

"That's true based on substantive issues," Dan retorted. "We're talking here about a topless waitress bar coming to town. The Clarion is not the National Enquirer. And until someone has a definite source with verifiable information, this story is in the can."

When no one else spoke, Dan said, "What else have you got?"

Sutcliffe cleared his throat. "The mayor and the city council just voted themselves a hefty pay raise. We're against that."

Dan said, "Agreed. Anything else?"

Claridge, another editor, spoke this time. "You don't mind when we're critical of your brother?"

Angry now, Dan shot back, "Of course not. My brother is a politician. We would be severely remiss if we agreed with everything he does. As long as the criticism is valid and professional, I have absolutely no problem with it. Is there anything else?"

Sutcliffe spoke. "No. That's it."

"Ok. Let's get to work."

When the meeting ended, Dan was left with the uneasy feeling that the editors wanted to say more but kept silent. There was an undercurrent of tension in the room that made Dan wonder what the editors knew that he didn't.

Chapter 7

On Friday afternoon Dan left the office satisfied that the week hadn't been all that bad, despite the tension between him and the editorial staff. He had a big weekend ahead and Dan was anxious to leave work and get on with it. Marla's high school graduation was Sunday. Dan and Rosalina were going to host a party for her. The guest list had already swelled to almost seventy-five people and counting. All the Kerr clan would be there as well as Rosalina's family, Bryant's and Marla's family on their father's side, the Salinas, and Marla's friends. Dan had a lot to do, and he wanted to get started.

Marla's prom was that night. Her date, Erik, was due to pick her up at seven. Then they would have the picture taking. Marla was still in jeans when Dan got home, but her hair had been done and she looked incredibly grown up. Marla was not a kid anymore. After the prom, Marla and Erik would go to a chaperoned gathering at the home of one of Marla's friends. Rosalina offered to cook breakfast for all of them the next day. Once the couple made their way to the big event, Dan decided he wanted to shop for some snacks for the party. Tomorrow would be too busy for shopping so off he went to the supermarket. A half hour later he returned with bags of chips, Doritos, Cheetos, nachos, bottles and cans of Pepsi, Sprite, and Mountain Dew. Just a few snacks became a grocery bill of thirty dollars. Rosalina just rolled her eyes.

Saturday was a long day of mowing and trimming, setting up tables and chairs, and Dan had to do the heavy lifting since Bryant was working. The day was hot, and Dan was forced to take frequent breaks during which he refreshed himself with his favorite brew.

At dinner that night, Dan and Rosalina ate alone. Bryant and Marla were both out on dates. The couple sat quietly absorbing the unusual silence. For most of his life, Dan had been surrounded by noise and family commotion. He didn't know quite how to feel, but he relished the privacy of a dinner alone with Rosalina.

The commencement was held in the stiflingly hot gym at the high school. The effect was the same as sitting in a sauna. So preoccupied was Dan with the temperature that he didn't realize Marla was ready to cross the stage until Rosalina whispered, "There she is."

Marla received two scholarships which astounded Dan and Rosalina. Marla had been a good student, but not an exceptional one. During her senior year she had been especially blase about her schoolwork and disdainful of teachers and the whole educational process. Yet she earned two scholarships. Dan wondered if the school had Marla mixed up with another student.

Everyone milled around after the ceremony. Dan and Rosalina met Erik's parents. Pictures were taken, hugs exchanged and soon it was over. All Dan could think about was changing into a tee shirt and shorts and grabbing a beer.

The graduation party was set to begin at four. Marla went to a party at a friend's house with the firm understanding that she would be home before any of the guests arrived for her party. The first guests to arrive were, appropriately perhaps, Mayor Kerr, his wife and two sons. Pup had offered to supply the beer for the party, but it was Dan who had to lift two cases out of the trunk of Pup's car. His Honor was under doctor's orders not to do any heavy lifting. Once the cases had been unloaded, Dan tried to engage his brother in convivial banter. Pup, ever the show man, droned on about his latest dust up with the city council. As he listened, Dan took the measure of his older brother who had gained at least fifty pounds since becoming mayor. His paunch was enormous, but usually hidden by well-tailored suits. Dan didn't miss the florid face and the beads of sweat at Pup's hairline. Pup chatted on obliviously, but to Dan he looked like a sick man, an accident waiting to happen.

A flood of guests arrived at the same time and the party was underway. Aunt Julia had sent word that she would arrive later to avoid the sweltering afternoon heat. The Salinas arrived with lasagna and wine, much to the delight of the other guests. Bryant and Marla's father arrived with his latest girlfriend on his arm. He and Dan shook hands amicably, but Dan was saved from having to converse as another wave of guests arrived. Bridy and Mr. Kerr slipped in through the back door. It had been decided earlier that Mrs. Kerr would not attend due to the suffocating heat.

The seventy-five or so guests dined happily on lasagna, sandwiches, salads, and pizza. No one seemed overly concerned about the heat since there was a plentiful supply of drinks to keep everyone cool. All was well until Stanley, well lubricated, grabbed

Mrs. Salina's arm and twirled her around like a Spanish dancer. When she recovered from her surprise, Stanley's dancing partner objected strenuously in English and Italian. "AAAYYY. Stunada, let me go. I only dance to music,"

"But Senora, I want to dance with you. I don't need music. A lovely woman projects her own sweet music."

Mrs. Salina flung him away with stiff arm followed by a boot in the ass. "AAAYYY, fenabla" was her parting salute.

Mrs. Salina's kick sent Stanley stumbling and he tumbled headfirst into the lap of the mayor. The two of them went head over heels as Pup's chair was upended by the force of Stanley's body. Sputtering and cursing, the mayor managed to get to his knees, but he had to be helped to his feet by Elaine and Bridy. He seemed unsteady and disoriented, but he soon found his voice. "Let me at him. I'll kill the son of a…"

Mimi cut him off with, "No swearing, Pup. There are kids here."

Stanley lay dazed at the feet of his father-in-law. Mr. Kerr watched in horrified silence as Gabby hurried over and grabbed Stanley by his belt. "Sit down, Stanley. You're disgracing me."

Stanley stared at his wife. "Wha' happened? Somebody tripped me."

Stanley had no sooner settled into a chair when Mrs. Salina approached and slapped him across the face. "Stunada. You make a fool of yourself and disgrace your wife. If you were my husband, I'd slap you senseless."

Stanley managed a lopsided grin. "I'd hate like hell to be married to you. Why don't you go back where you came from?"

Several people gasped at Stanley's last remark. Before anyone could react, Mrs. Salina picked up a wine bottle and swung for Stanley's head. Dan managed to intercept the bottle before Mrs.

Salina could inflict a fatal blow. "Why you stop me? I was going to do everyone a favor and kill him."

In the meantime, the intended victim reached for a bowl of punch behind him. The bowl was heavier than he expected and as he moved away from the table, the weight of the bowl caused it to tip, and a heavy flow of punch and sherbet landed squarely in Biddy's lap. Astounded, Biddy stood and screamed, "Stanley, you idiot. You just ruined my new Jordache jeans. They cost thirty dollars. I'll get you for this if it's the last thing I ever do."

Rosalina rushed to the rescue. "Come on, Biddy. We can wash the jeans. I'll give you a pair of my shorts to put on."

A hapless Stanley swayed, the now empty bowl in his hand was wrenched away by Cissy. "I spent all morning making this punch and now it's gone," she wailed. "Why do I bother to do anything for this family?"

"All right, Cissy. That's enough. Why do you have to make a federal case out of everything?" asked Bridy.

The rest of the guests stood around in stunned silence. Their astonishment increased when they saw Rosalina come out of the house with a police officer at her side. Rosalina pointed at Dan as though she expected him to explain the whole situation. Dan understood and approached the officer.

"Is there a problem, officer?"

"I was sent to investigate a report of a woman screaming," replied the officer.

Dan, himself a little tipsy, could hardly keep the amusement out of his voice. "Well, you see, officer. One of my sisters was yelling at my brother-in-law because he spilled punch on her new Jordache jeans. Then my other sister started yelling because she made the punch that my brother-in-law spilled into my sister's lap. That's what all the screaming was."

As if on cue, Aunt Julia and her caregiver, Ramona, appeared in the backyard. Noticing the police officer, Aunt Julia bellowed, "Why didn't you show up five minutes later? You could have given me a police escort to the party. I'd be the talk of the town."

The police officer looked around in complete bewilderment. Pup approached him. "Officer, as I'm sure you know, I'm the mayor. No. Don't eye me suspiciously. I really am Mayor Kerr. There's no problem here. If you knew my family, you wouldn't be the least bit surprised by any of this. Now, just head on back to your cruiser and rest assured, I'll put in a good word to the chief and let him know that you're doing your best to keep the streets of Coltonwood safe."

The harried officer turned to leave only to be confronted by Matty, Cissy's youngest son. "Officer, would you like a slice of pizza? You look hungry."

The officer knelt to the boy. "Thank you, son. But all I want is to get back to work. This is the craziest call I've ever been on."

After the officer left, people resumed chatting, eating, and drinking as though nothing had happened. Biddy reappeared in Rosalina's shorts. Stanley conked out on a chaise lounge. Aunt Julia savored her martini as she cradled Madison, Gabby and Stanley's youngest child. Most of the other children were terrified of Aunt Julia, but Madison snuggled happily in the crook of the thin, blue veined arm.

Dan noticed that Gabby was nowhere to be found and he went into the house in search of her. He surmised that she was upset by Stanley's behavior and didn't want to face people at the party. Gabby's wont was to withdraw when faced with trouble, and Dan had no doubt that she was holed up somewhere by herself.

He found her in Marla's bedroom, sprawled on the bed watching the party through the window. Dan's entrance surprised her, even though he tried to be as quiet as possible. Gabby spun around to stare at him. "Are you ok?" was Dan's tentative though silly question.

Gabby sat upright on the bed. "I'm embarrassed and disgusted. Stanley made a fool of himself and me. How can I ever face the family again?"

"Isn't that rather harsh? No one in the family will think less of you because of Stanley's behavior. He's responsible for his own actions." Dan knew he should not pursue this line of questioning, but he did. "Is everything all right between you and Stanley?"

After a deep sigh, Gabby replied, "Stanley wants to move back to New York. He says he misses the city. That's the last thing I want to do. I don't want to raise the kids there. I want them to have a happy life like we had as kids. That won't happen in New York."

"That's something you'll have to discuss with Stanley. Does he know how you feel?"

"Yes, he does, but when Stanley wants to do something, he won't listen to reason. It's all or nothing with him."

Not knowing how to answer, Dan remained silent. Gabby burst into tears and sobbed, "I miss Mum. I want to talk to her, to hear her voice. Why does she have to have dementia? It's like she's dead, but she's not dead. It's so unfair."

Dan gathered his sister in his arms. "I know, Gabby. I've asked myself the same question a million times. I sometimes read my diary to her, but there's no response. It's so sad and so frustrating."

Gabby withdrew from Dan and tried to compose herself. "I hate even visiting with her. It seems so pointless. My children will never know her. At least the other kids knew her as their grandmother, but my kids have been denied that. Well, I suppose we should get back to the party."

As they started to leave the room, they heard Stanley's muffled voice. "Sheila, where are you?"

Gabby took a deep breath. "I'm in here, Stanley."

Stanley poked his head into the room. "What are you doing in here?"

"I was so disgusted by your behavior, I just wanted to be alone. Are you sober enough to drive home?"

Stanley ignored the question. He looked at Dan with undisguised dislike. " I suppose you two have been having a heart to heart about me."

"It's none of your business what Chip and I have been talking about, Stanley. I asked you if you're sober enough to drive home. It's a simple yes or no question."

Dan excused himself abruptly. He didn't want to be in the middle of that argument.

The party was almost over by the time Dan returned to the backyard. People were filtering out. Marla had cut her cake and that seemed to be the signal that the party was drawing to a close. Pup accosted Dan. "Where have you been? I want you here when I present Marla with her gift from Elaine and me."

Oh, God, thought Dan. What will he give her? A trip around the world?

The gift turned out to be two tickets to a Guns N' Roses concert. Marla screamed and hugged her uncle and aunt. "I can't believe it. My favorite group. Oh, my God. Erik, Erik, we're going to see Guns N' Roses when they come to Boston. Oh, my God." The ecstatic graduate jumped up and down, unable to contain her joy. She hugged Dan and Rosalina still pumping her arms.

Dan was glad that most of the guests had left. Marla hadn't made a fuss about any of her other gifts, and the effusion about the tickets was becoming embarrassing. When the honored guest finally calmed down, she ran to Dan and Rosalina. "Mom, Dan. Thank you. No one ever had such an awesome graduation party."

Dan, drained by all the drama of the day, surveyed the yard. Fittingly, Aunt Julia and Ramona were the only people left in the otherwise empty backyard.

Chapter 8

Life quieted down by the end of summer. Bryant and Marla both left for college by mid-August. Bryant began his senior year and Marla her freshman year at UMass Amherst. Dan and Rosalina had the house to themselves and neither particularly liked the oppressive quiet that made the house seem so much bigger. Dan was accustomed to noise and controlled chaos having grown up in a large family. Without the kids, life seemed dull.

With no teenagers to fret over, Dan found himself preoccupied with Pup's health. His focus had shifted from worry about Pup's extracurricular activities to deep concern about his health. Dan could discuss his distress with Rosalina, but Pup resolutely refused to listen to Dan's admonitions about his health and lifestyle.

One late summer night Dan was trimming the hedge when Bridy surprised him. He hadn't seen or heard her approach.

"Hi, Chip. I'm walking to clear my head. Did I startle you?"

"Yeah. I'm getting too old for such scares."

"Sorry. I didn't want to pass by without saying hello."

"I'm glad that you stopped. I'd like to talk about Pup for a minute."

Bridy sighed. "What about him?"

"I'm really concerned about his well-being. He's obese and eating and drinking too much. He's right where he was when he had the heart attack. Remember the doctor said the next one would be fatal."

"You know that Put loves to tempt fate. Now that he's the mayor, he thinks he's invincible. He won't listen to Elaine or anyone else."

"That's what worries me."

"Pup always has to learn the hard way. Well, see you later. I want to get home before dark."

To Dan it seemed as if he was never free from the anxiety generated by his family. He kept telling himself that his siblings were adults and had to work out their own problems. He knew their issues were none of his business, and he didn't want to pry or meddle. Dan naively thought that the family angst had been buried with Champ. In reality, the problems loomed larger than ever.

Work was still a hassle, but at least when he was at work, Dan could try to forget the family troubles. Whenever he felt overwhelmed, Dan would reach for his diary: it had become almost like a drug for him. He now understood Rosalina's concern about his attachment to his journal. As much as he tried to focus on the present, the diary would draw him into the past, to a time when everything seemed better, at least to him. Yet he couldn't throw it out; it had become his lifeline whether he liked it or not.

Whenever he was stressed, Dan would retreat to his office, and take a few minutes to read the diary. Dan would amuse himself thinking about what entry he would read next. He always locked the door when he read. Dan did not want anyone on the staff to catch him reading a diary that he wrote as an eleven-year-old. Some would question his maturity, some his sanity.

Engrossed in thinking about what to read next, the buzz of his phone made Dan jump. Rachel said, "Mr. Murphy is on line one, Mr. Kerr."

In all the chaos within the family, Dan had nearly forgotten that his best friend John Murphy would be getting married in another week. The phone call jolted him back to reality.

"Hey, almost married man. Are you getting cold feet?"

"No way, Jose. Guys like me seldom get this lucky. I'm calling to tell you that we have a tux fitting on Friday at four-thirty. Is that a good time for you?"

"It's fine."

"Good. Then I'm thinking we can meet the ladies and have some dinner at the club."

"I'm all in. See you on Friday."

"Ah, Dan?" Dan felt his heart flutter at John's hesitation.

"Yes?"

"Remember you said that you wanted me to tell you any scuttlebutt that I heard about your brother?"

Another flutter. "Yes, I do."

"Well, I've been hearing a lot these days that the mayor is having a fling with a reporter at the paper. I'm sorry to be the bearer of bad news."

"You're only confirming what I've long suspected."

"It's pretty much common knowledge at city hall," affirmed John. "I'm telling you now, so I won't spoil everyone's dinner on Friday."

"I really appreciate that, John. See you on Friday."

Dan hung up and swore. It was true, after all.

Despite the sick feeling in the pit of his stomach, Dan summoned Laura Bridgewater to his office. The haughty young reporter sat and waited for her boss to speak.

"Thank you for coming, Laura. I won't keep you long, but I do need to ask you a question. Are you having an affair with the mayor?"

"Isn't that my business, Mr. Kerr?"

"I asked you a question that only requires a yes or no."

"Why are you questioning me? You have no right to be asking me what I do on my own time."

"I'll consider your lack of an answer to be a yes. Now let's get down to business. It's true, as you say, that what you do on your own time is your own business. Yet, in this case, your private life includes a public figure, the mayor. That changes things, don't you think?"

With a disdainful tilt of her head, Laura asked, "Are you trying to protect your brother? Is that what this Q and A is all about?"

Miffed, Dan answered, "I'm speaking to you as the managing editor of the Clarion, not as the mayor's brother. You would do well to remember that I'm also your boss."

"Are you going to fire me?"

"No, I'm not. I have no grounds, yet, to fire you. I also think you're a damn fine reporter, arguably the best on the staff. That being said, if your fling with the mayor becomes an issue, I will have no choice but to fire you."

Unimpressed, the young woman replied, "People don't care about these things. This is 1985 not 1955. Get your head out of the sand, Mr. Kerr. People are much more tolerant than they used to be."

"You are mistaken, Ms. Bridgewater. People do care about how public officials conduct themselves. Coltonwood may be a city, but in many ways, it remains a small town. People talk, rumors fly, and reputations get ruined. If you remember, the previous mayor was voted out because he had posters of rock groups in his office. People were angry and thought he was an adolescent, so they gave him the boot. It seems to me that you don't understand the community that you cover."

Incensed now, Ms. Bridgewater retorted, "I totally understand this town and its people. Now you're insulting me. I should quit right here and now."

"That's your decision, but first hear me out. People expect reporters to be impartial and nonjudgmental. You cannot write a story about the mayor and be impartial if your relationship with him is more personal than professional. To do so is to willingly deceive the people who read this newspaper. That is disingenuous and unfair."

"But..."

"Please let me finish. If the mayor gets himself embroiled in a scandal, you are involved as well. If that were to occur, I would have to fire you. If I fire you, I would also have to make full disclosure to any prospective employers who would contact me. Rest assured, I will not sugar coat any of this. You'd be lucky if you got a job with another legitimate publication."

With a show of false bravado, Ms. Bridgewater sputtered, "You can't blackball me because of what I do on my own time. I'll get a lawyer and sue the pants off you and this paper. This is so unfair. You wouldn't do this if I were a man."

Dan said, trying his best to be patient. "The situation involves you and a public figure. *The Clarion* pays you to write objectively and fairly, and if you cannot, then you should step down."

"But..."

Dan held up his hand. "I'm almost finished. Please remember that even if the mayor loses the next election, he can go back to his business. He will recover from whatever damage his relationship with you causes. You will not be so lucky. People will blame you and demand that you be fired. Then what? Do you have another job waiting for you? Are you prepared to endure the vitriol that people will hurl at you? It's the public's perception rather than the reality that counts in situations like this. I strongly advise you to be honest with yourself. You will be in deep trouble, and no one will be your friend. I'm serious about this, Ms. Bridgewater. Your fantasy world is about to explode, and you will be left to pick up the pieces. Starting tomorrow you will be a general assignment reporter. You're off the city hall beat."

Laura Bridgewater glared at her boss, her eyes wide. After a moment, she collected herself and stormed out of his office. "Screw you," were her parting words.

Chapter 9

Dan and John went for their tux fitting at the appointed time. John allowed himself a touch of vanity for his wedding; he chose a traditional black tux, but a shirt with a wing collar. His tie would be white while Dan's would be black. Both men were measured for suits and shoes.

At six o'clock Dan and Rosalina met John and his fiancée Jennifer for dinner. Dan was anxious to meet Jennifer and she did not disappoint.

"I'm happy to meet you both," was Jennifer's greeting to Dan and Rosalina. "John has told me so much about each of you."

Dan smiled. "I'm glad that I finally got to meet you. I was afraid John would wait until the wedding to make the introductions. He's kept you to himself for too long, don't you think?"

John had indeed been very quiet about his courtship of Jennifer. For a long time, Dan didn't even know of her existence.

During dinner Dan tried hard to be pleasant and engaging, but he kept replaying the scene with Laura Bridgewater in his head. In his mind, she had guaranteed her firing given the egregious disrespect she had shown as she left the office. She was the best reporter on the staff and would be hard to replace, but Dan couldn't tolerate such insubordination.

Dan had just taken a sip of excellent pinot noir and was about to take the first bite of his steak when John said casually, "I'm very happy that the mayor accepted the invitation to the wedding. I was afraid he might not want to come." Dan hoped that his face didn't show the disappointment he felt at hearing that Pup would be at the wedding. He had looked forward to the wedding as a chance to forget Pup and Laura and all the controversy surrounding them. It was just the distraction Dan needed, now even that was gone.

John looked around uncertainly after he spoke. "Is something wrong, Dan? Suddenly you don't seem happy."

Dan hesitated. He didn't want to spoil the occasion by mentioning the mess involving the mayor and the reporter or his obsession with the whole situation. He also didn't want to lie to his best friend. After another sip of wine Dan said, "You surprised me is all. I thought that the wedding was going to be just immediate family and a few close friends."

"For the most part, that's true," said John. "However, if not for the mayor I would not be where I am now. He fights for the funding of my job, and he's been a staunch supporter of the food pantry. I wouldn't have even met Jennifer if not for the mayor. I owe him a great deal."

"That's fine, John. I should not have even commented. You and Jennifer have every right to invite whoever you please to your wedding. I'm sure the mayor will have a blast."

"I hope so. We want our guests to enjoy themselves. This is one time the mayor can forget about being mayor and just be a regular guy. I'm sure the demands of his office get to him, and he needs a break."

Dan wanted to say that Pup was never bothered by being mayor. Being in office and in charge of a city was his lifeblood. Pup loved every minute of being mayor, even to the point of possibly sacrificing his family with his risky behavior. Dan only hoped that his brother had enough decency not to turn the wedding into a political spectacle, that he would only be another guest.

The two couples ate in silence until John abruptly said, "I'll surprise you again. I'm going to take my vows standing. I want to do that like any other man."

Dan gaped at his friend. "You're able to stand?"

"Technically no, I can't. But my physical therapist and I have been practicing this for months. I can lift myself up because my arms are so strong from wheeling myself around for so long. Jennifer will have hold of me to steady me. Then I'll have you as my back up. I even intend to stand for some pictures."

Dan marveled at his friend, the guy who had gone through so much, who worked so hard to better his life, to make something of himself. John Murphy was nothing short of amazing.

On Monday Dan checked his mailbox for Laura's letter of resignation, but there was nothing. He would have to give her the axe himself, as much as he hated to. He wasn't at his desk for five minutes when Laura appeared at the door.

"Mr. Kerr?"

"Yes, Laura. Come in."

The haughty demeanor was gone. Laura stood before her boss humbled and contrite.

"I want to apologize for my behavior and language on Friday. I was totally out of line and I'm sorry. Do you want me to resign, or will you fire me?"

Her wide brown eyes scrutinized Dan's face, who remained silent. He wanted to make her sweat. Finally, he said, "I don't intend to fire you or demand your resignation. I do want an apology, however. I'm not excusing your behavior so I'm going to suspend you without pay for three days. Of course, now you have two strikes against you. Any more breaches of protocol will not be tolerated."

The relieved reporter said, eyes downcast, "Thank you, Mr. Kerr. You're a good man. Anyone else would have given me the boot."

Dan dismissed the compliment with, "I want to ask you again if you're involved with the mayor."

Laura remained mute.

"Once again, your silence says it all. I've given this matter a lot of thought, as I'm sure you have as well. You do realize that the mayor is using you to garner favorable publicity."

At that Laura flared, "He is not."

"I'm afraid that you're mistaken, Laura. Grant me this. I know the mayor better than you do. He's a political animal through and through. He will do whatever is best for him to ensure his reelection. It's very likely he's bought you nice things, sent you flowers, wined and dined you, out of town, of course. This is all a show to ensure your loyalty. Once he's safely reelected, he'll drop you like a hot potato."

Laura regarded her boss furiously. "None of this is true," she lashed out. "The mayor is going to leave his wife to be with me."

Dan had all he could do to restrain his incredulous laughter. "And you believed him? You're even more naive than I thought. He has no intention of leaving his wife. You can forget that right now.

You're just a convenience now so you'll give him good publicity. He's just using you. Don't you understand that? I reassigned you to save you from being hurt as you will eventually be if you continue to see the mayor. Do you still wish to remain in the employ of the *Clarion*?"

After a long pause, Laura said quietly, "Yes. I do want to stay."

"Fine. That will be all Ms. Bridgewater."

To clear his head after the tiring exchange with Laura. Dan sought out his diary to read what he had written about Neil and Mimi's wedding:

The big day has finally arrived. Drama Queen #1 will soon be out of my hair, for in three hours she will become Mrs. Neil Mullaney and will begin her new life in a nearby town. I can hear the reedy voice of the bride to be as she's screaming for the rest of the female family members to hurry. They all have an appointment with the hairdresser to put on a face for the day. The hairdresser is opening her shop an hour and a half early to accommodate Mimi, Mum, and the rest of the bridal party.

At last, I never again have to hear on almost a daily basis Mimi's complaining about shoes, caterers' estimates, bridesmaid's dresses, invitations, photographers, flowers, the list is endless. I sometimes wonder why she and Neil just didn't run away and get married, but I know the reason: Mimi loves to complain, and she loves having all the attention focused on her. She's been in heaven these last few weeks. Maybe I could have been able to bear all of this with more patience, if I wasn't the only member of my immediate family who is not in the wedding party. I'm still upset even though everyone has been telling me not to be upset. It's not fair. I don't care what they say.

As I begin this entry in the diary, I turn my attention to scheming to get Drama Queen # 2 married. Maybe she will fall in love with the best man, and they will run off together after the reception. Maybe she will dance with one of Neil's relatives or friends and start going out with him. Getting her out of the house would be wonderful since she complains even more than Mimi.

Finally, I slinked out of bed and began dressing in the new suit Mum and Dad bought me. Big deal. I'd much rather be putting on a tux like Pup and Champ. Champ and I share a room, and I saw him examining various parts of his junior usher "costume."

"What's this?" he asked, holding up what looked like a belt a wrestler might wear.

"How do I know? You figure it out."

Champ gave me one of his blank looks and called downstairs, "Dad!"

Dad bounded up the stairs, probably afraid he would have to confront the day's first crisis.

"What's the matter?"

Champ held up the belt.

"That's a cummerbund," said Dad.

"A what?"

"A cummerbund. You wear it around your waist. I guess it's meant to hide the suspenders."

"I have to wear suspenders," wailed Champ.

"They're just part of the wardrobe when you wear a tux," explained Dad. "Now hurry up and get ready before the photographer gets here."

Champ stood bewildered with the cummerbund in one hand and the bow tie in the other. "Can you help me, Dad?"

Dad has to be the most patient man in the world. He just looked at Champ and said, "Let's start with the pants and shirt. I think you can manage those."

Champ was fine until he found the black buttons. "What are these?"

"Those are the pearl stud buttons that go over the buttons on the shirt. I'll put them on for you."

Dressed, Champ looked pretty good, but he was fidgeting and shifting from foot to foot.

"Dad," he finally said. "What do I do when I'm at the church?"

"You offer your arm to a lady and walk her to a seat."

"Just ladies?"

"Oh my God, what an imbecile," I thought. He can't be serious, but he was. I almost asked Dad if I could wear the tux and be the usher and let Champ be the altar server. At least I know enough not to escort a man down the aisle.

Distracted by this fascinating conversation, it took me a minute to realize that Pup had emerged from his lair and was standing in the bedroom doorway. He looked great and again I felt the unfairness of my older sister in not choosing me as part of the wedding party. To be fair, she did ask me to serve the wedding and I said yes, but now I regret that decision.

Pup ignored Champ and me and looked directly at Dad. "Dad, you better come downstairs. Biddy got into the Bosco, and she's got it all over herself and her hair."

We all ran downstairs to find Biddy covered with chocolate sauce. Her fingers, face, and hair were all smeared. Dad merely sighed and picked up his youngest daughter and placed her in the tub. He ran the water and immersed her in soapy water. Biddy loved being bathed and she had absolutely no idea that she was the first crisis of the day.

Dad said as he shampooed her hair, "Bid, I'm going to remind you of this on your wedding day."

Champ appeared in the doorway and whined, "Dad, tell me again what I have to do."

From the tub Biddy yelled, "Champie scared."

Champ was too nerved up to even react to Biddy who was now splashing water in his direction. I can tell Dad is at the end of his patience. He growled, "Have Pup show you what to do at the church."

What an imbecile.

The ladies returned, Biddy was clean, the bride was dressed and ready for the photographer. All four grandparents came to the house for pictures and then they all rode together to the church. I sat on Grampy's lap since there was no room in the back seat for me. I was low man again.

Saba was already there when I arrived with my "costume" for the wedding – my cassock and surplice. I lit the candles and the two of us arranged the kneeler and the chairs in front of the altar for the couple, the maid of honor and the best man. I couldn't help but look at the people filling up the benches. Pup was taking a lady to her seat. Champ evidently figured out what to do. He was taking Aunt Sue to her seat. There I was just watching.

Saba, Father Power, and I were standing in front of the altar when Pup and Champ took Mum to her seat. I'd seldom seen her look more beautiful or relaxed as she did right then. I've heard people say that a bride is radiant, but in this case, the bride's mother was radiant. I had no idea she'd be so happy to be rid of Mimi. As for Pup and Champ, both looked fantastic in their white tuxedos with the pink carnations in the lapels. Once again, I was mad and jealous.

Here comes the bride. I have to admit, Mimi did look better than I ever could have imagined. Even veiled, she was beautiful as she slowly made her way down the aisle on Dad's left arm. He was looking at her and smiling slightly. I wonder if he was thinking about this morning with Biddy. The church was so quiet that I could hear the slight rustle of Mimi's gown as she approached the altar and Dad gave her hand to Neil. Now they were only a few feet from me; I could see the look she gave Neil and the look he gave her. Was this really my constantly complaining sister? Has being with Neil actually changed her that much?

As much as I have hated being the only member of my immediate family who was not part of the wedding party, I had to say that being so close to Mimi and Neil as they took their vows and exchanged rings was cool. Mimi's voice was barely a whisper as she repeated after Father Power. Neil's voice was strong but not loud. As Neil lifted her veil to kiss her, I could see that my sister was truly happy. I was puzzled by the strange feeling I had over my heart. Only I saw Mimi and Neil at this moment. Suddenly I didn't care that wasn't wearing a tux.

I was included in the picture taking outside the church. I'm wearing the new suit. All around me people were saying what a beautiful wedding it was. I couldn't wait to get to the reception since I was starving.

We all headed to the reception hall in a long line of honking cars. I saw some kids I know on Main Street, and I waved to them. They actually waved back. I saw Johnny M. hanging around near the Spa. I didn't wave to him, but I looked back and saw him watching the procession with a funny look on his face. My joy didn't last because I remembered that Anthony and Girard would be at the reception. I didn't want to spend the reception and the party after hanging around with them. Crazy cousin Aggy will be there but so will Bobby Salina and Bart, thank God. Bobby and I will somehow have to avoid Anthony and Girard, but it won't be easy.

I was thrilled to sit with Gram and Gramp, Uncle Jerry and Aunt Irene, Uncle Clement, my cousin Kip, who I hardly know, and Aunt Julia. I made a beeline for the table so I could sit next to Aunt Julia. She's my favorite aunt because she doesn't waste my time asking me about school like so many other adults who don't know how to converse with kids. I never know what Aunt Julia might say, but she's never dull. There she was. Her dress was a purple thing with feathers around the collar. Her hat looked like Captain Crunch's with decorations like birds or maybe apples. Her greeting to me was typical, "Hi Chippy. How's tricks?" I had no idea what that meant, but I liked the sound of it.

"Hi, Aunt Julia. Did you like the wedding?"

'Yes, it was nice, but weddings are all the same. I've been to a million of them." To which Uncle Clement said, "She's talking about the number of times she's been married."

I thought about the day in school when I wrote about Aunt Julia being a grass widow. But now she was talking to me again.

"Do you still want to be a writer when you grow up, Chippy?" asked Aunt Julia.

"I still want to be a writer."

"Oh? What kind of writer? Newspaper, magazine, books?"

"Books."

"Well, that's very good, but most writers starve while writing a book. Do you like to read?"

"I read all the time, Aunt Julia."

"Have you read that book **Peyton Place**?"

I was shocked. Mum would never let me read that book.

"How do you like my hat?" *Aunt Julia never pursued any subject for any great length, but I was surprised at how quickly the topic changed.*

"I like it," I lied.

"You know, I bought this in a very expensive shop on Fifth Avenue in New York. My second husband pays me a lot of money, so I can buy nice clothes. Most women in America don't know how to dress. Ladies in England know a thing or two about fashion. You know, the Queen Mother is famous for her hats."

Gram saved me this time. "You did a beautiful job on the altar today, Daniel."

"Thanks, Gram." I was pleased by this. Gram never gives anyone a compliment unless she really means it.

Uncle Jerry, who up until now had not said a word, turned to Aunt Julia.

"Julia, did you know that Lizzie Cassidy is in the hospital again?"

"Good place for her," hissed Aunt Julia. "What is it? Cirrhosis of the liver?"

"You've never been known to throw it over your shoulder, Julia," said Aunt Irene. She sounded a little mad.

"Well, Lizzie freezes and eats it. I've never been that bad," said Aunt Julia.

What were they talking about? Freezes and eats what?

Our conversation stopped as the bride and groom cut the cake. Neil pretended to smash the cake in Mimi's face as the guests kept hitting their glasses with forks so Neil and Mimi would kiss. Weddings can be very boring.

Pup danced with Angelina Salina. Did I mention that I think she's the most beautiful creature on the face of the earth? I love the way her name rhymes. I wish I was Pup. I'd love to dance with her. She, of course, has no idea I'm in love with her. She has more boyfriends than Mum has dresses.

After dinner, I was free to find Bobby and Bart since none of us was interested in dancing. We left the banquet hall to get away from the music. The lobby was cool with a huge circular staircase and windows on all sides. Just when I looked, my idiot cousin Anthony was sliding down the railing of the staircase. Bobby and I both hoped he'd fall and land on his head. Bobby can't stand him because Anthony calls my buddy Bobby Saliva instead of Salina.

"Hey, bat head," Bobby yelled to Anthony. "Are your rabies shots up to date?"

Anthony was leaning forward riding the banister like it was a horse. When he heard Bobby's insult, he sat up and fell to the right of the railing. He tried to save himself with his legs which caused him to fall into the stairs, his arms and legs going in all directions. That move caused Anthony to rip his pants entirely up the back. Bobby and I couldn't stop laughing and ran outside to hide from Anthony who'd be looking for revenge. When we went back inside, we saw Anthony wearing white pants; someone in the kitchen loaned him a pair of pants that the cooks wear. How uncool. Poor Anthony. I wondered if Girard would get himself a pair so they can be a matched set.

The wedding was more fun than I thought it would be. Bart, Bobby, and I left the reception hall and chased each other around the parking lot, shirttails out of our pants, ties lost somewhere. My new shoes hurt my feet. I wished I could go home and get my sneakers, but it was too far to walk. I couldn't ask Dad because he was having too much fun. The last time I saw him he was dancing some silly dance called the Hully Gully. Totally stupid. I don't like weddings once the dinner is over. Dancing was not my thing. I was glad it was nice weather. I'd be bored out of my head if I had to stay inside. Gabby came out to get us, saying that Mum wanted us inside for Mimi and Neil's last dance. When I got back in, Mimi and Neil had changed from their wedding *clothes to regular clothes. Going away clothes is what Grammy calls them. Everyone at the wedding was now in a circle around the couple as they danced one last time. I walked behind everyone so I could get next to Aunt Julia. She wasn't wearing her hat anymore. She was red-faced and dancing before the music even started. That lady knows how to have fun. She put her arm around my shoulders and pulled me close to her. "Someday, Chippy, this will be you dancing with your bride."*

"But, Aunt Julia," I said. "I'm only twelve."

"Time flies, Chippy. I remember Mimi when she was just a baby. Now she's a married woman."

Just then Drama Queen #2 came running over. "Aunt Julia, I caught the bouquet. I'll be the next to get married. I'm so excited."

Me too. I hope that prediction comes true as soon as possible.

Now it was time to say good-bye to Mimi and Neil. I felt funny. Yes, I'm glad she's married and on her own, but for some reason, I'm also sad. When Mimi came to me, she hugged me. "Thanks for serving my wedding, Chip. Neil and I really appreciate it."

"Ok." I couldn't think of anything else to say.

We all followed the newlyweds to their car. I saw Pup minus tux and tie with a can of shaving cream in his hand. He and Champ sprayed "Just Married" all over Neil's car. They also tied cans to the rear bumper. Aunt Julia then produced a bag of rice which she and several other people began throwing at the car. Neil and Mimi drove away in a shower of rice with cans bouncing behind the car.

Not a bad wedding after all.

Dan picked up his tux Friday afternoon; the wedding was at six that evening. With an effort of will, Dan was able to put aside his preoccupation with Pup and Laura. He was determined to enjoy the evening and be fully present for his friend.

Dan and Rosalina rode to the church with Pup and Elaine. Dan was nervous but elated. He kept checking his pocket to make sure he had the rings. Since he donned his tux, Dan's mind kept returning to the night of his senior prom. He felt the same delightful apprehension as he had on the June night many years before as he anticipated spending the night partying with his friends.

Dan met John at the church. They could do nothing but fidget and wait for Jennifer to arrive. The guests filtered into the chapel as Dan wheeled John to the front of the pews and soon Jennifer made her way down the aisle on her father's left arm. John and Jennifer joined hands as Jennifer's father and Dan lifted John's wheelchair above the two steps that led to the altar.

When the time came for the exchange of vows, Jennifer and John faced each other and John slowly pushed himself up from his wheelchair. Jennifer clasped his hands, and she pulled as John pushed. After a few wobbly seconds, John stood. Dan moved the chair to one side and took his place directly behind John just in case he lost his balance. He didn't. John stood erect and strong as he spoke his wedding vows. He and Jennifer exchanged rings then kissed as they became husband and wife.

John eased back into his chair and the ceremony was soon over. Dan pushed John as he and his new wife processed out of the chapel to the spontaneous applause of their guests. A limo provided gratis by Callahan Funeral Home brought the newlyweds to the reception where they greeted their guests during a cocktail hour prior to the dinner.

In his toast, Dan praised his friend and lauded his courage and determination. Instead of the speech he had been practicing, Dan spoke extemporaneously. "I know that all of you join me in wishing John and Jennifer all the best as they begin their life together. I've always admired John but tonight my admiration has turned to amazement, to wonder. I raise this toast to the most inspiring man I've ever known and to his lovely wife. I know they will be able to overcome whatever challenges they face. To Mr. and Mrs. John Murphy, may you know an abundance of happiness and joy. You both deserve it."

A string quartet played as the guests dined on rare roast beef, au gratin potatoes, and sauteed summer vegetables. The champagne flowed. John and Jennifer cut the cake, which was then served as dessert. Jennifer decided to forego the throwing of her bouquet. Instead, she presented it to John's mother and a similar one to her own mother.

As the evening ended, Dan, ever the journalist, summed up the wedding in two words: pure class. Everything had been perfect. Pup even enjoyed the evening as a guest. He didn't try to turn the wedding into a campaign event, much to Dan's relief. After coffee and good-byes, the couple entered the limo to a shower of rice. They were off for their honeymoon in Antigua.

Dan basked in a warm glow of contentment until he and Rosalina prepared for bed. It was then that she told Dan that Elaine had confided to her that she was convinced that Pup was having an affair. Reality slapped Dan in the face once again.

Chapter 10

Dan went to work on Monday still smarting from Rosalina's revelation about Pup and Laura. He and the editorial board would meet at nine, so Dan didn't even have time to calm himself with the journal. The editors were irked that Dan had reassigned Laura Bridgewater without their knowledge or consent. As the managing editor Dan felt that under the circumstances, he acted within his authority. While he could ignore the board, Dan could not ignore His Honor. Pup called him in a barely controlled rage.

"Why did you reassign Laura Bridgewater? Don't you care that I have to face a reelection soon? Laura always gave me good press. The moron who took her place can't tie his shoes. How could you do this to me?"

"Calm down, Pup. Now I have a question for you. Are you having an affair with Laura?"

"That's my business, not yours. Even if I am, that's not a good reason to reassign her."

Once again, Dan knew the truth from an evasive answer.

"Need I remind you that you're a married man with kids? What if Elaine finds out? Doesn't that concern you?"

"Look, Chip. What I do is my business. Period. It doesn't concern you or Elaine or anyone else. Obviously, that's the real reason you reassigned Laura. Are you trying to sabotage me? That would make a great headline. 'Mayor Stabbed in Back By His Uncaring Brother'. Thanks for nothing."

The conversation with Pup rattled Dan so much that he left the office to have a coffee at Zippy's. As he sipped his decaf, he made a sudden decision to visit his mother. When he arrived at the nursing home, he was greeted by Gabby and Bridy who were also visiting. Dan felt a qualm when he saw his sisters. Was something wrong? They reassured him that that their mother was fine. Mrs. Kerr did look more alert and perkier than usual. Dan gave his mother the customary peck on the cheek after which he made small talk with Gabby and Bridy.

"How's Stanley?" Dan asked Gabby. Not that he cared.

"He's fine," was the icy response. "Can't you ever be nice when you ask about Stanley?"

"What's wrong? All I did was ask about him. Next time, I won't say a word."

"It's the tone I don't like."

"A thousand pardons. You know he's my favorite brother-in-law."

Gabby shot him a look but said nothing. Mrs. Kerr's hearing was fine, and Gabby did not want to upset her mother.

Dan addressed his mother. "So, Mum. John's wedding was great. I didn't forget the rings or drop the glass during the toast. You would have been proud of me."

Mrs. Kerr's expression remained unchanged, so Dan regaled his sisters with all the details of the wedding and reception. As he was speaking, Mrs. Kerr interjected plainly, "I want you kids in the house before dark."

Startled, Dan asked, "What, Mum? What did you say?"

There was no reply to his question. The sisters and Dan exchanged incredulous looks. Had their mother really spoken? The moment came and went so quickly that they weren't sure that their mother had spoken at all.

Dan felt a migraine coming on, so he avoided the office and headed home. As he drove, he wondered what his mother would think if she knew about Pup. He had always been her favorite. No doubt she would not believe a word against Pup, or she would try to rationalize his behavior. Once home, Dan secluded himself in his bedroom with the shades drawn and his head under a pillow. It was all getting to be too much: his mother's illness, Pup's outrageous behavior, the animosity at work. Part of him wanted to resign and move out of town. His rational side told him that he had to face his problems, not avoid them. He just didn't know how.

When his head cleared, Dan felt the urge to talk to Mrs. Salina. He needed to unburden himself to a sensible person who would really listen. Before he could leave, the phone rang.

"Chippy. I haven't talked to you in ages. Would you like to take me shopping? I haven't done that in ages either."

Dan sighed. "Hi, Aunt Julia. I'm fine," he lied. "I can't take you shopping now, but we can make a date for that."

"Oh, goody. I haven't had a date in ages either. I'll wear a special outfit. Which of my hats do you like best?"

At Aunt Julia's mention of a date, Dan's mind groped with a long dormant memory of something Champ had said about Aunt

Julia. What was it? Maybe it was in the diary. He would have to check. It was.

That night at dinner I remarked to Mum, "Mum, did you know Aunt Julia has a boyfriend?"

Mum looked amused. "She does?"

Champ then blurted out, "What are you, stupid? Who would go out with Aunt Julia?"

"Champ don't call your brother stupid. You know you're not supposed to use that word."

"Sorry, Mum. Sorry, Chip."

Not to be outdone, I announced, "I even know his name."

Dad looked up. "Oh, yeah. What is it?"

"Jack Daniels."

I saw Mum and Dad look at each other and Dad almost fell out of his chair laughing. Mum looked instantly mad. "I don't find that funny, Bert." Dad couldn't stop laughing and the rest of us laughed even though we had no idea what was so funny.

Mum put an end to this. "All right, kids. Time to do the dishes, then homework."

A few days later, Mum informed me that I had to take over Champ's paper route.

I was stunned. "Why?"

"Well, Champ has practice after school, and he won't have time to do it. You're old enough now to take it over."

When Dan was able to connect with Mrs. Salina, her greeting was typical. "AAAYYY. Why are you here? Is it your mother?"

"No. I just wanted to visit you and talk. I saw my mother this afternoon."

"I know you want coffee. I have biscotti and tiramisu. That's all I got."

Dan selected a biscotti while Mrs. Salina settled herself to hear why Dan had decided to visit.

"Mrs. Salina, I had to talk to you. My head is spinning with everything going on in my life."

"Is your mother worse?"

"No. She's the same. My biggest concern is Pup."

"What about him?"

"I strongly suspect that he's having an affair with a reporter at the paper. He's also eating and drinking too much. He's out of control."

Mrs. Salina grinned wickedly. "Ha. I'm a sidekick, you know. I named him Pup when he was a baby. I knew he was trouble even then."

"Do you mean psychic? You said sidekick."

"You know what I mean. Talk to me."

Dan took a deep breath and began. "I know I should mind my own business, and I need to stop trying to be the family watchdog, but I can't help it. You know that I idolized Pup when I was growing up. It kills me now to see what a degenerate he's become. He doesn't care about his family. He's become so self-absorbed he's losing touch with reality. I'm really afraid something terrible is going to happen."

Mrs. Salina stared at Dan for a long time, seemingly at a loss for words. She placed her hands around her coffee cup and spoke softly. "You have to let Pup take the fall. There's no other way. Maybe it will take another heart attack, maybe his wife will throw him out. You won't be able to stop whatever happens. Pup is a stunada, just like my girls. I can't do anything with them. You can't do anything with Pup. Let it go."

Mrs. Salina's advice was just what Dan had expected. He knew she was right, but she didn't tell him how he was supposed to just stop worrying and obsessing about Pup. Dan's mind had become a black hole, and he had no idea how to climb out. Dan had enough self-knowledge to know that he was a nurturer; he liked to take care of people. Yet, oddly enough, this cone of caring had shrunk to only include Pup. Dan took little notice of Cissy's nervous compulsions, of Gabby's insecurity, of Biddy's overall neediness. In his opinion, only Bridy had the brains and the confidence to find her way in life. Dan admired his younger sister. She didn't waste her time or energy worrying about Pup or any of her sisters. He wished he had Bridy's common sense and intelligence.

Deep inside, Dan knew that he had to plumb the depths of his own motivation. Was he trying to protect Pup or himself? Did he expect Pup to remain the nearly perfect football hero of his imagination or was he ready to accept Pup as he was, a flawed human being like everyone else? Dan had only questions and no answers. As for the diary, Dan knew he had to keep it close. He was far from ready to throw it into the fire.

The day came for Dan to take Aunt Julia shopping. He would rather have a root canal than go clothes shopping, but he had to make good on his promise. Aunt Julia was elated when Dan picked her up, excited as a child by the prospect of a trip to the store. Once Dan had Aunt Julia settled in the car and the wheelchair in the trunk they set out.

"Where would you like to go, Aunt Julia?"

"Jordan Marsh, of course. That store has the best clothes and the best salespeople."

"Ok. To Jordan Marsh we go."

The ride was quick, then Dan had to retrieve the wheelchair and plunk Aunt Julia into it. He was almost out of breath when he finished and resolved for the hundredth time to start working out and getting in shape.

The grande dame of stores was as imposing as ever as the dome came into view. Dan wheeled Aunt Julia to the women's dresses. She poked through the racks but didn't seem interested in any of them. Eventually, a young salesclerk approached tentatively. "May I help you?"

Aunt Julia got right to the point. "Young lady, do you have any dresses that are appropriate for someone my age? All of these dresses are too young for me."

Clearly, the clerk had never dealt with someone as old as Aunt Julia. "Well, this is all we have for dresses. Most women prefer pants now, except for special occasions."

"Special occasions," retorted Aunt Julia." I wore a dress every day of my life until recently. Women just don't know how to dress any more. This is disgraceful. This store has gone to hell just like all the others."

"Not completely," replied the naive clerk. "We still sell our famous blueberry muffins."

"Blueberry muffins," spat Aunt Julia. "I came here for clothes, not food. The very idea. Chippy, take me home."

During the ride home, Aunt Julia held forth. "This world has gone to hell in a hand basket. No one cares about style or manners. Where can I shop if Jordan Marsh doesn't have any clothes that I want?"

"But, Aunt Julia, you have plenty of clothes. You don't need anything new. Is there any other store you'd like to try?"

"No. I'm tired. I'm just remembering when you could get a good cup of coffee at Woolworth's at the counter. You can't even get a good cup of coffee anymore."

"A lot of places have good coffee. Would you like a cup? We can go to the drive up at Dunkin Donuts."

"Drive up? What do you mean?"

"You give your order and then drive up to the window, get your coffee and pay and be on your way."

"Really? I never heard of such a thing. But no. I'll skip the coffee. It gives me palpitations anyway."

Aunt Julia lapsed into silence and her demeanor worried Dan. Seldom was Aunt Julia quiet for long. She had an opinion about everyone and everything, and she was not shy about expressing her sentiments.

"Are you ok, Aunt Julia? You seem unusually quiet."

"I'm fine. I was just thinking that I'm almost ninety-five."

Dan grinned. "I know. I hope you live forever."

"Well, I don't. At my age, all my friends are dead or in a nursing home. I have to depend upon other people if I want to go anywhere. If I didn't have Ramona, I would be in a nursing home."

"I hope you live to be a hundred. My life would be pretty dull without you."

"You know, Chippy, there are worse things than death. I'm lucky that I still have most of my marbles, but what will happen if suddenly I don't? I've seen a lot in my life, the good and the bad. I always looked nice even when I wasn't working any more. My tank is pretty much empty. I don't mean to be morbid, but that's the truth of the matter."

Dan had never heard Aunt Julia speak so frankly. Was she trying in a roundabout way to tell him she was ill?

"Are you feeling all right, Aunt Julia? Have you seen your doctor lately?"

"That god damn quack is counting the days until I die. He has no idea who I am, nor does he care. I treat myself now. Who the hell needs him?"

Dan breathed a little easier. This was Aunt Julia being her usual feisty self.

"Don't give up on your doctor so easily, Aunt Julia. If you don't like him, go to someone else. You do need a doctor to monitor your health."

"No, I don't. Jack and I have worked well together for many years. No need to change now."

After Dan had brought Aunt Julia home, he realized that she hadn't wanted to go shopping at all. She wanted to talk, to tell him what she had probably not confided in anyone else. Dan vowed to visit more often or to call. Aunt Julia had always been a strong woman, but now age had made her vulnerable and Dan very sad.

Chapter 11

Autumn came quickly and the days got shorter. Mrs. Kerr's condition remained the same and Pup kept a low profile even as he campaigned vigorously for reelection as Coltonwood's mayor. Most of the infighting between the editorial board and Dan had stopped since the paper endorsed His Honor. Dan enjoyed the Pax Romana, but he knew hostilities would resume once the election was over.

One day in late October Dan received a call from the mayor. They had not spoken in over a month. Dan was still incensed about Pup's affair with Laura Bridgewater, and the mayor was furious with Dan for meddling in his private life.

"Hey, bro," began His Honor. "I've put aside four tickets to my reelection victory party for you and your family."

"Thanks, but how do you know that we want to go?"

"You are my brother."

"I'm glad you finally noticed. Rosalina and I will go."

"What about the kids?"

Pup really was clueless, thought Dan. "They're both away at college, remember? They're not going to come home for one night."

"Oh, right. I forgot. How stupid of me."

"I'll say. Feel free to call any time."

"Are you still pissed at me, bro? There's no reason to be."

"Pup, we've had this conversation. Good luck with the election. I'll see you at the party."

"Don't forget to bring your wife," sneered the mayor.

"I could say the same to you and mean it more."

Dan hung up, frustrated as ever with his intractable brother. Whatever progress Dan had made with accepting his brother's behavior had just evaporated. Pup's cavalier attitude towards the family infuriated Dan no matter how much he tried to rationalize it. He decided the less he talked to Pup the better.

Election Day was chaotic at the paper. Every reporter had been assigned to cover the election. Dan and everyone else knew that Pup would win in a landslide, but both campaigns had to be covered. Worst of all, Dan knew that Laura Bridgewater would be history once the mayor was reelected. She had made a smooth transition from covering city hall exclusively to reporting on other events in Coltonwood.

Mayor Kerr declared victory a half hour after the polls had closed. He roundly trounced his opponent, a young, inexperienced newcomer to the political scene.

Dan and Rosalina showed up at the victory party fairly late. The office was very busy preparing the next day's edition and Dan had to stay until the election coverage had been put to bed. By the time he got home to fetch Rosalina it was after ten.

The party was loud and energetic. His Honor was ebullient as he thanked his supporters. His victory speech was so impassioned that Dan feared his brother might suffer a massive coronary. Pup waved his arms, gesticulating in all directions. He pounded the podium and screamed into the mic. It was a performance for the ages.

Now that the election was over, Dan could concentrate in earnest on preparation for his favorite holiday, Thanksgiving. Whenever he had a spare minute at work, he would jot down menu times or create guest lists. He wanted to have a huge affair and cook some dishes he had never attempted. So carried away was he that when he looked over the guest list, he counted forty people, way too many. Yet, if they had dinner at the church hall with its spacious seating and well-equipped kitchen, he could pull it off. Thanksgiving made Dan dream big dreams, most of which were totally unrealistic. He decided to consult his diary and remind himself how Thanksgiving had been when he was eleven.

Gramp insisted we walk even though it's freezing cold. We knew the reason. He wanted to smoke his cigar on the way to the store. The A&P is only about a block away, but on a cold day, it seems much farther. Gramp tried to divert us with war stories from WWI, but I was the only one who seemed to be interested.

I love the A&P. I love the smell, the layout of the store, the people who work there; everything about it. Gram sent us with a shopping list. We had to buy two oranges, two bananas, two apples, and one bunch of red grapes and one bunch of green. We also had to pick up olives, pickles, and cranberry sauce. The store was mobbed. It was so crowded it was hard to move around. There were so many people that I had a hard time getting to the coffee machine. We were not buying coffee, but every time I'm in the store, I stand by the coffee machine as someone grinds the beans into coffee. I love the smell.

Reading this excerpt from the diary made Dan even more anxious to begin the preparations for the big dinner. On the day before the holiday, Dan only worked a half day so he would have the afternoon to work at a much more pleasant job. A few days earlier, Bridy had called and asked if he would show her how to cook such a big meal. The two of them met at Dan's house and peeled, cut, and chopped, talked about old times and sipped an excellent cabernet. Mid-afternoon the phone rang.

"Hey, bro. What time is dinner tomorrow?"

Startled, Dan said, "Why aren't you in Texas?"

"I didn't go this year. Elaine and the boys went without me."

"How come? You always go to Elaine's family for Thanksgiving."

"I decided to take a year off. I'm really tired from the campaign and my doctor is worried about my blood pressure. He recommended that I not fly. Besides, I want to go to the game which I haven't done in over a decade."

Dan knew that everything Pup had just said was a bald lie, except the part about the game.

Impatient as always, Pup persisted. "So, when is dinner?"

"One o'clock."

"Do you want me to bring anything?"

"No. Just your vainglorious self will be enough."

"What is that supposed to mean?"

"Nothing. See you tomorrow."

"Who else will be there?"

Pup never knew when to stop talking.

"Cissy and Carl and their boys, Gabby and her wonderful Stanley and kids, Dad, Bridy, Aunt Julia if she's well enough, Rosie, the kids and me."

"A fair assembly. See you tomorrow."

Dan wondered how Pup knew the words, 'A fair assembly.' He must have heard someone say them. He couldn't have come up with that on his own.

"That was Pup," Dan told Bridy. "He's coming to dinner tomorrow."

"He's not going to Texas? Why?"

"The lie he told me is not even close to being believable. He's tired and his doctor doesn't want him to fly because of his blood pressure. Pure invention. He and Elaine will no doubt be splitting soon."

Bridy looked up from the carrots she was peeling. "I hoped that Pup would come to his senses and give up his paramour. He's such an idiot to be so cavalier about his wife and family. He'll live to regret his foolish behavior."

Dan hesitated then equivocated. "It's really not surprising. He puts politics and his own pleasure above his family. Elaine is probably sick of it."

"I think you're right. It will be a different Thanksgiving with Pup here."

"Yeah. Too different for my taste."

Dan was deeply disturbed by Pup's phone call, but he kept his tone light and bantered with Bridy as they prepared the vegetables.

When Bridy left, Dan opened a beer and braced to tell the whole story to Rosalina when she got home. Then Dan remembered that Bryant and Marla were both coming home from college later in the afternoon. That night the family sat down to a dinner of Chinese takeout per order of Bryant and Marla. After dinner both kids went out with friends and Dan told Rosalina over wine that Pup would be coming to Thanksgiving dinner.

Chapter 12

Dan got up early on the holiday to prep and cook the turkey. He slid the 27-pound monster into the oven at 2:30 and went back to bed. However, sleep eluded him as he thought about Pup and his affair with Laura. The news from Pup should not have come as a shock, but Dan was stunned by the realization of his greatest fear. As much as he groped to understand Pup's behavior, he just could not come to grips with the certainty that Pup and Elaine were finished mostly because of a young, fetching reporter who worked for Dan, who castigated himself for not firing Laura when he had the chance.

Worst of all, Dan was distraught that Pup had become such a facile liar. How could Pup speak of his broken marriage as though he was discussing a daytime soap opera? Had Pup's egotism eroded his decency and his morals? Was there any hope for him?

After an hour of depressing thoughts, Dan slipped out of bed and picked up his diary, which he kept in his briefcase, carefully concealed from Rosalina. The journal usually afforded him comfort, but not this time. He felt guilty that he had to read it in secret, afraid that his wife would castigate him for wallowing in the past. Dan knew that his dependence on the diary was as adolescent as a kid reading the same comic book over and over. He wondered what unacknowledged need kept him chained to the journal. Dan usually felt the diary's tug in bad times, but Thanksgiving memories were among his happiest. So why was he holed up in the den reading about Thanksgiving as he had numerous times before?

As soon as I opened the door to Gram's, I could smell the turkey cooking and feel the warmth of the house. I ran upstairs to leave my jacket on the bed and went straight to the kitchen where Mum, Aunt Julia, Aunt Irene, and Gabby were sitting around the kitchen table. Mum put her wine glass down with a thump when she saw me.

"Is everything all right? Is the game over?"

"Everything's all right." I lied, not about to tell Mum that Pup had been hurt. "I left early because I was freezing. Dad and Champ are still at the game."

I looked at the clock and it was almost noon. The game should be over now.

"Hi, Dan."

I turned around to see my cousin Bart standing there. I had completely forgotten that he and his family were going to be with us for Thanksgiving. The last time I saw him I was at Mimi's wedding, but I didn't pay much attention to him then. I thought he was strange, and his sister Aggie was even stranger. What could I say to this stranger who happens to be my cousin?

"Hey, Bart." Not a bad start. Now what do I say?

Gram saved me. "Daniel, could you check to see if all the hot plates are plugged in?"

"I'll help you," said Bart.

As I was checking the plugs as instructed, Dad and Champ walked through the dining room to get to the kitchen. Champ's face was beet red from the wind and the cold. He was walking stiff legged like he couldn't feel his feet. I wanted to make a comment, but he looked so awful, I just kept my mouth shut.

Dan had a dinner to cook for fifteen people; he couldn't spend another minute fretting about Pup. He showered quickly and donned his favorite decade old jeans and his old college sweatshirt. Comfort was necessary. When he got downstairs, Rosalina, Bryant, and Marla were at the table eating breakfast. No one looked up to greet Dan. He poured himself some coffee and sat. "Good morning," he said, louder than necessary.

Rosalina poured some Raisin Bran into a bowl and passed it to him. "All set for the big day?"

"I guess so. All the prep is done. Now it's show time."

Rosalina said, "Are you still worried about Pup?"

Dan preferred not to discuss Pup in front of Bryant and Marla. At the mention of Pup, Bryant suddenly found his voice. "Is Uncle Pup coming? Doesn't he usually go somewhere else?"

Dan sighed. Now there was no avoiding the issue. "Yes, he's coming alone. The rest of his family went to Texas."

"Cool," exploded Bryant. "Uncle Pup is great. I can't wait to talk to him."

Marla swallowed a gulp of milk. "Uncle Pup is, like, a total bore. He's totally full of himself."

This remark drew a reprimand from Rosalina. "You will not speak of your uncle like that. Show some respect."

"I'm just expressing my opinion," sniffed an indignant Marla. "I am allowed to do that."

"I merely asked you to show some respect."

"Whatever."

Dan ate his cereal and pretended to read the paper, but his mind was a jumble of cooking times and Pup worry. He needed to calm down or he wouldn't be able to get anything done. Rosalina, perceptive as ever, said, "You're still worried about your brother, aren't you?"

"Yes, I can't seem to focus on anything else. It infuriates me how much he dominates my thoughts. I just can't seem to let go."

"Maybe so, but you need to concentrate on the task of feeding fifteen people who will be expecting dinner."

"I know. I know. I'll set the table."

But when Dan entered the dining room, the table was completely set.

"Who did that?" he asked Rosalina.

"Marla and I did it while you were in the shower."

"Thanks, but what can I do now?"

"Let's peel the potatoes."

As they worked, Rosalina chatted and Dan's mood gradually improved. He chuckled inwardly when he thought of Marla's description of Pup, a bore. She was, like, correct.

Bridy arrived at noon and the two of them set about cooking Brussels sprouts, candied yams, and mashed potatoes. Rosalina abandoned the kitchen for her recliner where she sat engrossed in a book. Dan poked his head into the living room and asked,

"How can you be so calm when a house full of people will be here in less than an hour?"

"Why not? I'm not the cook. By the way, did you buy any pies?"

Dan swore and hit his forehead so hard it hurt. How could he possibly have forgotten pies for Thanksgiving? He had only one option. He called Mrs. Salina.

"AAAYYY. What you want? You burn the turkey?"

"No. I forgot the pies. Do you have any extras?"

"Stunada. Of course I have pies. My daughters all with their men today. Just Salina and me."

"Come here. You can eat with us."

"AAAYYY. We have a reservation at a restaurant."

"Cancel it. Please come here."

"When?"

"Now!!"

Fifteen minutes later, the Salinas arrived with three pies and a dozen bottles of homemade wine. Dan desperately wanted a glass of red, but he didn't trust himself to drink and cook at the same time. Dan took the turkey out of the oven and was amazed at how golden brown it looked. He delicately carved the breast. The meat was tender and juicy. Mrs. Salina brandished a wooden spoon in Dan's face. "AAAYYY. What size is that buzzard?"

"Twenty-seven pounds of succulent turkey perfectly cooked by moi."

Mrs. Salina instantly deflated Dan when she said, "You have to make gravy. Turkey is no good without gravy."

Dan cast a hapless look at his neighbor. "Where do I start? Mum always made the gravy."

"AAAYYY. Allow me."

Dan heard a car door slam, then nothing, then a pounding on the door. Pup's indistinct voice yelled, "Chip, open up." Dan did so only to see Pup holding Aunt Julia in his arms.

"What the…" gasped the ultra-surprised Dan.

"Hi, Chippy. It's been a long time since I was carried over the threshold by a handsome man."

Befuddled, Dan just stared as Pup carried Aunt Julia into the living room. Pup returned in a moment and said, "I'll explain in a minute." Presently, Pup returned with Aunt Julia's wheelchair. "It's easier to carry her than to get this thing with her in it up the steps." Pup, red faced and sweating, eased the chair into a corner, out of the way.

"You scared me for a minute. I thought Aunt Julia had fallen. Now I can see that it would be easier to carry her."

Wiping his brow, Pup said, "Yeah. She's light as a feather. The chair weighs more than she does."

Pup then spied Mrs. Salina. "Francesca, are you here to give Chip cooking lessons? That's good. The rest of us won't have to worry about being poisoned."

"AAAYYY. Look who's talkin.' I bet you can't boil water."

His Honor grinned. "I'll bet that you are correct."

It was a difficult business to herd everyone into the dining room for dinner. The guests had been subdued by Salina's wine and the chicken wings that Pup had brought. Bryant waited until just about everyone had been seated. He wanted to sit next to Pup, his newest idol. Dan smiled as he remembered how he would do the same thing so he could sit next to Aunt Julia. Dan noticed that Rosalina kept glancing out the window. She was looking for the absent Marla. "Where could she be?" the worried mother asked Dan.

His answer did little to console Rosalina. "Who knows? She's a teenager. She could be anywhere."

Just as Dan began to say grace, Marla burst through the door. "I went to my friend's house. Sorry I'm late." The tardy teen didn't look the least bit repentant. She knew from the look her mother gave her, that she was in for it later.

Rosalina went to the buffet first to fill a plate for Aunt Julia, whom Pup had carried to the table. The nonagenarian sat at the head of the table where she could preside over the dinner. Cissy looked around and asked, "Where's Dad?"

Dan explained, "He's having dinner at the nursing home with Mum. Didn't you know this?"

Cissy sniffed. "Obviously not or I wouldn't have asked."

After he had heaped his plate, Bryant talked rather than ate. "Uncle Pup, what position did you play in high school?"

Pup, pleased by the prospect of talking about himself, glowed. "I was a defensive back most of the time, but I was also a wide receiver. In the last game of my senior year, I got hurt."

"How? What happened?"

"The guy I was lined up against came at me at lightning speed. I felt like I'd been hit by a freight train."

As Pup spoke, Dan remembered his own reaction when he saw Pup on the ground on that freezing cold Thanksgiving many years before as recorded in his diary:

Dad, Champ, and I left for the game about nine-thirty. Since Pup plays for the high school team, we don't have to buy tickets; we just show the guy at the gate the pass and in we go. The place was mobbed.

Eventually we found seats and the wooden bench felt like a block of ice. I could feel the cold right through my jeans. I wished that I had worn a hat. My feet were slowly freezing and the game had just started. I decided that I would leave as soon as I'd seen Pup in the game for a few plays. I looked at Champ beside me. He was so absorbed in the game; he didn't realize how cold it was sitting there. Suddenly he was jumping in the air. Pup had just caught a pass and taken a vicious hit. Pup was on the ground and not getting up. My heart was pounding. Was he all right? Would he walk again? Why didn't he get up? Everyone around us was standing and quiet. The doctor ran out to where Pup was down and knelt beside him. I thought that it was a good thing that Mum wasn't there. Her greatest fear had always been that Pup would get hurt playing football. She would probably run onto the field if she was here.

The doctor and the coach helped Pup to his feet. His helmet was off, but he appeared to be ok. He walked slowly to the bench. At least he wasn't being taken to the locker room. I realized that for the time that Pup was on the ground, I forgot that I was cold. Once Pup walked to the sideline I was freezing again.

At half time, Dad stood up and said that he was going to the locker room to check on Pup and we were to stay where we were, no roaming around the field. Dad returned with hot chocolates for both of us and the report on Pup. "He's ok. He just had the wind knocked out of him. I don't want either one of you to mention this to your mother. Is that clear?"

"Luckily, I never got hurt playing football," offered Bryant. "I got plenty of bumps and bruises, but nothing serious."

The conversations lapsed until Bridy said nonchalantly, "I want everyone to know that I've decided to go to law school."

"That's great," gushed Pup. "It will be good to have a lawyer in the family. You can defend Chip when he gets sued for libel."

"Very funny, Pup. Ha, ha. I think you'll end up in a courtroom before I will."

Cissy chimed in sweetly, "Why don't you look for a husband, Bridy? Don't you think you're a little old to be going back to school?"

Bridy refused the bait. "What I do with my life is no business or concern of yours, Cissy. People go to law school at all ages, for your information."

"I still think you should get married and have kids."

Aunt Julia reached across the table and placed a hand on Cissy's. "Cissy, dear, you must remember that you and Bridy come from different generations. Women now want careers. They delay marriage and motherhood, and that's not necessarily a bad thing. I should have been a lawyer, but in my day, women didn't even think of such things, much less pursue a career. What Pup said is right. It will be good to have a lawyer in the family. You never know. I might just take the plunge again and make another mistake like I did four other times. Then I'll really need a good lawyer."

Everyone at the table laughed heartily at Aunt Julia's comment. Matty, Cissy's son, not understanding the joke, looked around bewildered. "Uncle Chip, why is everyone laughing? What's so funny?"

Chip had to take a healthy gulp of Salina's wine before he could answer. "Never mind, Matty. Aunt Julia's jokes aren't meant for anyone under the age of eighteen. She wouldn't understand any jokes that you might make. It's ok."

"Excuse me," muttered Cissy. "I have to have a cigarette."

When his mother was safely out of ear shot, Matty said to Dan, "Mommy's mad again. Why is Mommy always mad and then having a cigarette?"

Dan had no idea how to respond to his nephew. He didn't want to disparage Cissy, nor did he want to tell Matty that he was wondering the same thing. Clearly, Cissy was battling her own demons, but how could he explain that to a child? Dan didn't want to lie or mislead Matty, so he changed the subject. He pointed at Mrs. Salina and asked, "Do you recognize the lady who gave you the cannoli a few years ago?"

"AAAYYY. No cannoli this year, just pies. No one to bake for anymore. My daughters are only concerned with looking good for these men they chase. Stunadas."

After all the time he spent cooking, Dan realized that the guests had finished in less than ten minutes. No one offered a comment or even mentioned the food until Rosalina raised her wine glass in Dan's direction. "My compliments to the chef."

As if on cue, everyone else echoed, "My compliments to the chef."

No one had left the table even though the meal was over. Pup capitalized on the lull by addressing his second youngest sister, "Bridy, have I got a deal for you."

"Frankly, I'm leery of any deal involving you," was his sister's reply.

Nonplussed, His Honor continued. "I think you'll like this. I'd like you to consider becoming the director of the food pantry."

Bridy was astounded as was everyone else. "Is this a joke? Did you fire John Murphy?"

"No joke. I did not fire John. But he's so busy with the other aspects of his job that the food pantry has become too much for him. What do you say?"

Bridy looked thoughtful for a moment. "You do realize that I need to study to prepare for the law school aptitude test? I have to take the test in May, so I need time to prep."

"No problem. The food pantry is a part-time position. Even while you're there, you could study since there is a lot of down time."

"I can't do any heavy lifting."

"Again, no problem. There are still plenty of volunteers. Your job would be to monitor the amount of food going in and out and to supervise the volunteers. There are guys who unload the food."

"Let me think about it. When would I start?"

"ASAP. This Thanksgiving put John over the edge, so you would have to start immediately in anticipation of the Christmas rush."

"I need to sleep on this. Can I let you know tomorrow?"

"Of course. You know I'm on the job 24/7."

Eventually, the men retreated to the living room to watch football, but the women remained at the table with Aunt Julia presiding.

"I think I would have been a cracker jack lawyer in my younger days. No judge would dare to tell me I was out of order. I'd take on anybody, even Clarence Darrow. I had the proper clothes for the courtroom also."

"But you couldn't wear a hat in the courtroom," Cissy reminded Aunt Julia.

"They would make an exception for me," was the pithy reply.

Dessert and coffee were consumed quickly. Aunt Julia asked Pup to take her home since it was time for her date with Jack. The mayor conveyed her out as he had brought her in - in his arms. The other guests soon asked for their coats and extended their thanks and farewells. Another Thanksgiving was in the books.

The next day, Dan called John Murphy and asked his friend if they could meet for coffee at Zippy's Coffee Shoppe downtown. John quickly said yes. After an exchange of pleasantries, Dan got down to business. "Have you heard anything about Pup and Laura?

Pup's wife went to Texas without him. Pup denied any trouble, saying his doctor didn't want him to fly."

"I haven't heard anything new. The rumor mill at city hall has been unusually quiet. I saw Laura the other day. She was covering an event at my church. Otherwise, I really don't see either one."

"Good. Yesterday Pup offered your job at the food pantry to my sister Bridy. She's a good choice. She's bright and sensible. For once Pup was using his head."

John looked pleased, but added, "Will she accept? I really don't have time for the pantry. I'd love to see a good compassionate person in my place. Would she be there for the duration or just on an interim basis?"

"Bridy wants to start law school next year. She can do it before then, but I don't know about afterwards."

John sighed, "Something's better than nothing."

Chapter 13

After an all too brief Thanksgiving break, Dan returned to work ready to enjoy a honeymoon of sorts with the editorial board. Since Mayor Kerr had been reelected by an overwhelming majority, the board had no fault to find since the paper had endorsed the mayor for a second term. A fragile peace would prevail until after the inauguration when the board could once again resume hostilities. But Dan was wary now that Pup had planned to appoint Bridy to replace John Murphy as the director of the food pantry. The editorial board would excoriate the mayor for nepotism in its most blatant form.

Dan called Pup to voice his concern about Pup's plan to appoint Bridy to replace John. The brothers talked and Dan proposed that Pup hold off any official announcement until the new year. In the meantime, Bridy would be just another volunteer all the while learning the job from John.

"That's a good plan, Chip," Pup conceded. "Bridy's a quick study. She'll know everything before Christmas."

"True," agreed Dan. "But you had better be ready for war when you announce the appointment."

The mayor chuckled. "No big deal. I've been there before. Now that I have your ear, I'll tell you about my plans for December. I want to have as many events as possible between now and Christmas, and I'd like the paper to cover all of them."

"Yes, boss. It can be arranged."

His Honor called a few days later agog with excitement. "Elaine and I are going to host an open house a week before Christmas. You and Rosie are invited."

"Who else will be there?"

"The council and the school committee, department heads, the superintendent of schools; all the elite of Coltonwood will be there."

"And are you going to use public funds to pay for this extravaganza? That would really please the common folk who reelected you."

"I'm going to take the money from the rainy-day fund."

"Isn't that supposed to be for emergencies? More fallout from the paper if you do that."

"No problem. You and the other bigwigs at the paper will be there."

"Ok. But what do you have planned for the average taxpayer? What do you intend to do for them?"

The mayor laughed, obviously delighted with himself. "That's the best part. We'll close Main St. so people can walk around. All the stores will be open. There will be hot drinks and food available. It will be called the Coltonwood Christmas Spectacular. It will be awesome. More details to follow."

The mayor called Dan just about every single day with more elaborate plans for the celebration. As a journalist, Dan could see that all this effusion was a diversion to distract the taxpayers and make them forgive any charges of nepotism the Clarion would surely level against the mayor once Bridy's appointment was announced. Dan knew it was a political ploy, but a good one.

The mayor was at times beside himself with excitement. "Chip," he foamed. "City hall will be open for the Spectacular and some ladies from the women›s club will be selling blankets and hats and scarves. These ladies like to knit and croquet."

"Pup, that's crochet, not croquet. Croquet is a lawn game."

"Oh, yeah. Whatever. People will love that stuff to give as presents. This is going to be the best thing to ever hit Coltonwood. It will become an annual tradition. I'll go down in history as the mayor who brought the whole city together."

"Yeah. Maybe someone will erect a statue of you in solid gold in front of city hall."

"That would be a fitting legacy for Mayor Kerr."

"You would think so."

"You bet I do."

Poor Pup, thought Dan. He really meant it.

The Coltonwood Christmas Spectacular lived up to its name. Hordes of people strolled Main St. and visited the local businesses. Dan and Rosalina walked arm in arm amid the many families, seniors, and everyone in between. A light snow was falling, which gave an almost magical feeling to the evening. The mayor, with Elaine on his arm, was in full campaign form. He kissed babies and ladies, shook hands with every man he met. He stopped in every business along his way. Bundled up against the cold, His Honor resembled a grizzly bear enjoying the freedom of being beyond its habitat.

For his part, Dan felt a wave of nostalgia wash over him. He remembered the pre-Christmas days of his childhood when everyone went downtown to do their shopping. Most of the stores from that time had long since closed, but there were still many stores trying desperately to hang on in the wake of the boom of malls. Dan was determined to stop in at all of them, many of which he had never patronized. There was one, a women's dress shop, that he never had any reason to enter until tonight. He was astounded to find that the store had a lower level with household items.

As he walked slowly along with Rosalina, Dan thought about the Christmases of his childhood, especially Christmas Eve which was always spent with the Salinas. First there was the skating party at the man-made pond behind the Salinas' house, then the party inside where everyone dined on the seven fish Mrs. Salina prepared in the old Italian tradition. Dan groped in his mind for what he had written in his diary about that night. He would read it later.

The skating party has been going on for years. Even though it was only about twenty degrees, most of the people in the neighborhood were there. Pup and his new girlfriend glided around the ice. Champ showed off his skating moves as usual. Gabby, however, tried to stand up on her skates. Two other teenaged girls helped her by grabbing each of her arms and having her skate along with them. Sofia, who really doesn't like Gabby, was looking back and smiling as though Gabby was some invalid who needed constant help. If Sofia wasn't a girl, I'd hip check her into the tall grass beside the pond. There is a brook that runs behind the pond and Bobby and I skated so far away we couldn't hear anyone on the pond. We don't know how far the brook goes, but it was scary at night, so we decided to go back.

The ice was really crowded now, and Mum and Dad were skating and holding hands. When they skated into view, I couldn't believe the happy, carefree look on Dad's face. So different from the frazzled look he usually has, especially at work. Mum, too, looked young and worry free. I watched and wished they could do this more often.

As I was doing another loop, Bridy, my annoying sister, skated up beside me. For an eight-year-old, she's really a very good skater.

"Chip?"

"What?"

"Is Santa Claus real?"

This caught me completely by surprise. Why didn't she ask Mum or Dad? Why me? Then I remembered that I was about her age when I realized that there is no Santa Claus. I also remembered how sad I felt. Annoying as she can be, I still would like her to have one more Christmas believing.

"Yeah, Santa Claus is real. Why are you asking me this?"

"I heard some kids at school say that there is no Santa Claus, that it's your parents who put the presents under the tree. Is that right?"

"Nope. They're wrong."

"How do you know?"

I had her attention then. "I know because I saw him once."

I could tell by the look on her face that she wanted to believe me, but she wasn't exactly sure.

After a minute she said, "You're lying."

"Am not. I really did see him. You know that we don't have a chimney, so Santa has to go around to the front door. I was looking out my window at Bobby's house when I heard the sleigh land in the backyard and Santa came around the house to the front. I didn't dare

leave my room because if Santa hears anybody up in the house, he won't leave any toys. After a while he came back out the door and I saw the sleigh cross the street to Bobby's. Seeing is believing, you know."

"Has Pup seen Santa?"

"Maybe. Why don't you ask him and let me skate?"

Bridy smiled slowly. "Yeah. Seeing is believing."

Mission accomplished.

The night was getting colder and colder, and a lot of the neighbors left the ice for the food and the warmth of Mrs. Salina's house. I wanted to stay and skate.

Now the biggest event of the season was to take place at Pup's and Elaine's home: the bash to entertain the movers and shakers of Coltonwood. Dan and Rosalina picked up John and Jennifer Murphy and made their way to the party. Their plan was to spend an hour or so then go to a restaurant for a quiet dinner. The mayor greeted them with alacrity. He was resplendent in a black tux and a wing collar, reminiscent of a maître d in a swanky restaurant. The mayor glowed as he shook hands with Dan and John. "Come in, gentlemen. The party is in full swing."

Once inside, John was surrounded, and someone put a beer in Dan's hand. No sooner than two sips later, Dan was accosted by a city councilor. "Good to see you, Dan," said the pol, his hand outstretched.

"Merry Christmas, Al. It's always a pleasure to see you," lied Dan.

"Yeah, but sometimes your paper has too much to say. Could you tell the editorial board to ease up a bit?"

Dan frowned, feigning ignorance. "What do you mean?"

"You know what I mean - that editorial about some councilors being unresponsive to their constituents concerns."

"Why do you take offense? You're a politician, Al. You're fair game for the paper. Besides, there have been complaints from some people. We don't invent these issues. There were no names mentioned. You need a thicker skin, my man."

Dan strolled away to find Rosalina, no easy feat since the house was packed with people. He couldn't even see John. He did see Elaine who was as radiant as her husband. If there was friction between them, neither showed it. Both were born hosts, and they were in their element and loving every minute of it.

"Hi, Dan."

"Hi, Elaine. Have you seen Rosie?"

"I did when she first came, but not since. I can't even find my husband, and he's hard to miss."

Dan did his best to plunge through the sea of humanity when he felt a tug on his elbow. Next to him was the former mayor, and Rosalina's boss.

"Hey, your honor. It's great to see you. Are you still running the family business? Do you still have those Kiss and Alice Cooper posters?"

The former mayor grimaced. "Yeah, in the cellar. I am running the business, but I don't have full control. My dad wants to retire to Florida, but he can't seem to let go."

"Why not? You ran a city. I think you can run a business."

"So do I. I want to run for mayor again. I loved the office, but I think your brother will probably be the mayor for the rest of his life. I wish I had been this popular."

"He does love being the mayor. Why not run for another office? You know the ropes."

"I do now. I was too young when I was mayor. I didn't have much of a clue."

"You may have been young, but you did a good job. Rosalina loved working for you."

"I'll be she did. She covered my butt more times than I care to admit."

Dan's reply was interrupted when he was abruptly pulled to one side by another city councilor. "Hey, what do you think you're doing?"

The assailant, well lubricated and loud, didn't mince words. "Look, Kerr, your paper needs to call out the mayor for appointing his sister to a city job. If that's not patronage, I don't know what is."

Dan had to take some deep breaths to control himself. "Have you discussed this with the mayor? You're on the council. You and the others will have a say on the matter. Go find some fool who's willing to listen to you. Excuse me."

Dan's blood pressure was rising. He just wanted to find Rosalina and the Murphys and get the hell out to relax with his wife and friends and daydream about the approaching holiday.

Christmas Eve was spent with Mr. Kerr, Bridy, Bryant, Marla, and the Salinas. Dan ordered a steamship roast and flexed his culinary muscles with a medley of roasted winter vegetables. The meal was supplemented by several bottles of Salina's homemade wine. Recent Christmas Eves have been bittersweet for Dan for many reasons, not the least of which was his mother's illness and the family instability. Dan also sorely missed the skating party and the Italian Christmas Eve custom of the seven fish. Mrs. Salina had given up the fish several years before, and now she and Salina even ended the much smaller wine and cheese party.

"I really miss the old Christmas Eves," Dan said to Francesca. "We all looked forward to the skating and the eating."

"AAAYYY. I had to stop. It was just too much. I was hoping one of my useless daughters would take over and keep it going, but they are all too lazy. What could I do? I had to stop."

"All good things do come to an end," sighed Dan. "Things change. The neighborhood is different now, a lot different. Do kids still skate on the pond?"

"Of course. We like to have people around since Salina and I fight so much. I look out the window and remember the good old days."

Suddenly Bryant piped up. "Why don't we skate tonight? The ice should be hard enough. It's not too cold. That would be cool."

Dan was elated. "What a great idea. Who's in?"

"I am," said Bridy. "I'm the best skater in the family. Champ was the second best. Call Pup. He might like to go."

Dan was now all fired up. He called Pup who agreed to come in half an hour. Even Mr. Kerr agreed to try to skate if he had strong arms to hang onto him. It was then decided that whoever wanted to skate could and then they would return to the house for coffee and dessert. Marla was not happy since she had plans with friends but said she would skate for a few minutes.

Pup arrived alone. "Elaine's a Texas girl. She doesn't even own skates," was his explanation for Elaine's absence. Soon the entire entourage made its way up the street to the Salina's house. The back lights were put on and everyone took to the ice. Mr. Kerr had a tough time at first, but soon found his sea legs and could skate alone. Bridy showed off by skating on one skate with one leg in the air. Dan and Rosalina glided smoothly as a couple and Dan was reminded of his parents who would skate the same way. Pup got off to a slow start, his girth and his general lack of exercise hindered his progress. After a few falls, he found his rhythm and began to enjoy himself.

The night was perfect. It was cold but not freezing. Numerous constellations of stars studded the sky. Dan's heart felt light, an unfamiliar sensation of late. He daydreamed as he skated of Rosalina's reaction when she would open her present from him and see the reservations for a cruise in February. He smiled as he pictured her shock and then delight.

Eventually, everyone got tired and returned to Dan and Rosalina's house for coffee and dessert. Mrs. Salina had made cannoli, tiramisu, and Italian cookies, all of which were devoured with rather indecent speed. Marla left to join her friends, but Bryant remained and looked wistful as he listened to the chat about Christmas Eves past. When everyone had left, Dan asked Rosalina if she would like to open one present. She demurred since Marla wasn't there, but Dan insisted. "Ok," she sighed. "Just one." Dan had put the paperwork in a gift box to make the present look like jewelry. Rosalina was puzzled when she saw folded papers, but then screamed when she read them. "Oh, my God. A cruise. Thank you, thank you, thank you, Dan."

"You are most welcome, my love. Merry Christmas"

Chapter 14

On January 6, 1986, The Honorable John Francis Kerr was sworn in as the mayor of Coltonwood for the second time. Flanked by his two sons, Pup placed his left hand on the Kerr family Bible that Elaine held and swore to uphold all the laws and statutes incumbent upon him. After he had kissed his wife and hugged each son, Pup began his second inaugural address which he delivered in precise, measured tones. Gone were the podium pounding and the wild gesticulations that marked his first speech.

As the mayor spoke, Dan pondered the enigma of his older brother. Pup had been an indifferent student at best. His only real interests had been football, girls, and beer. He had no desire to attend college, but he did learn carpentry from their maternal grandfather and eventually, after his military service, started a successful business. Now he stood in the august chamber of the city council, the chief executive of their hometown. True to form, Pup defied conventional wisdom and achieved a goal that had seemed totally beyond his reach. The incorrigible Pup had traded his work boots for wing tips, to the surprise of many except himself.

Dan snapped out of his reverie long enough to hear Pup speak of their father. He told the crowd that his father had owned a small business in the city. "My father was able to support a large family because the good people of Coltonwood supported him. Now the malls and the big chains are doing their level best to destroy small business, but my administration is determined to keep small businesses in the city thriving. That is my pledge to the people who work for themselves."

Dan's thoughts drifted again, this time to his mother. Pup had always been her favorite even though she and Pup vehemently denied what the other Kerr kids knew to be the truth. How proud she would have been to see her oldest son as the mayor of the city. All of the Kerr clan sat proudly listening to Pup speak, but his mother who lived shrouded in the shadow world of dementia, had no idea that her oldest son was now beginning his second term as mayor. Mrs. Kerr had endured the disappearance and death of her second son, and now she was denied the chance to savor the honor that Pup had brought to the family. Dan's heart and mind recoiled once again at the unfairness of life.

"I refuse to make empty promises or guarantee that life in Coltonwood will be utopian during my administration," the mayor told the crowd. "All I promise is that I will do my best every day as mayor to ensure that the people of Coltonwood will get a fair deal. Remember, my door is always open. You don't work for me. I work for you. I will do my best each day to justify the trust you placed in me. Let's get to work."

The applause was sustained and loud as the new mayor drifted into the audience, shaking hands, and acting every inch the politician. It looked to Dan as if Pup had been born to govern Coltonwood.

A brief reception followed the ceremony. Dan got some coffee and pastry and decided to return to work. Inauguration Day was a busy day for the paper. Dan had assigned a cadre of reporters to cover the swearing in of the new mayor so there would be plenty to do when he returned to his office. He would see the whole family at night when the Inaugural Ball would be held at a local hotel. Thus began the second term of Mayor Kerr.

The weeks following the inauguration were long and tedious. Dan spent an inordinate amount of time daydreaming about the cruise he and Rosalina would take in the first week of February. He would catch himself lost in a reverie even during meetings at work. So excited was Dan that he bought a lot of new clothes and even joined a gym to shed some excess holiday pounds. Every day after work Dan would faithfully workout, motivated by his new wardrobe and the relaxation the awaited him on the cruise. Realistically, he knew he would probably lose interest in the gym after the trip, but he might find the impetus to continue even then.

One evening Dan left the gym for home in yet another light snowfall. It had snowed three nights in a row. Dan looked forward to relaxing in his recliner with a good book. He was comfy and deep in a book when the phone rang. Dan paid no attention until Rosalina hurried into the living room.

"It's a lieutenant something. He wants to talk to you. He says it's urgent." Dan picked up the phone.

"Hi, Dan. This is Charlie Watkins. I'm sorry to tell you this, but your brother the mayor has been involved in an accident. He hit a tree on Boundary St. It's bad. He's in the ambulance now on his way to the hospital. The female passenger has yet to be extricated from the car."

Stunned, Dan thanked Charlie and turned to Rosalina. "Pup and Elaine have been in a car accident. Charlie says it's bad."

"Both of them? Oh, my God. Should we check on the boys?"

"Right now, I'm going to the hospital."

"I'll go with you."

Dan and Rosalina arrived at the hospital in a few minutes despite the steady snowfall. Dan's mind couldn't quite grasp what had happened. He couldn't imagine the impact Pup's accident would have on the family. He and Rosalina waited in a room where the overly loud tv squawked an asinine game show. Dan wanted to throw a chair at it to silence it. He and Rosalina held hands as they waited for what seemed an eternity for news about Pup and Elaine. A doctor finally appeared. "Are you the family of Mayor Kerr?" He looked about fifteen years old.

"We are," replied Dan. "What can you tell us? Are my brother and sister-in-law dead?"

"The mayor is alive, but he has sustained a traumatic head injury. We suspect that there may be some paralysis involved. We're sending him to Boston by ambulance tonight for further evaluation."

"What about my sister-in-law? How is she?"

The doctor looked puzzled. "The mayor was the only patient transported to the hospital. Perhaps she was taken to another hospital. Are you the responsible party who can sign the papers giving permission to transport the mayor?"

"Well, I guess I am if his wife isn't able to do so." Dan signed the necessary paperwork, affixing his signature without reading a word. He and Rosalina decided to go home and to process what had happened and try to find out Elaine's whereabouts. Once home, Dan realized that he had not called his father. To his immense relief, Bridy answered the phone.

"Bridy, it's Chip. Pup has been in a car accident. He's being sent to Boston for more evaluation. The doctor said he has a traumatic head injury and could be paralyzed. Elaine was with him, but we don't know where she was taken."

Dan heard a gasp and a sharp intake of breath. "Oh, my God. How could this happen? What will I tell Dad? Do you want to talk to him?"

"Not now. I want to find out where Elaine is and what her condition is."

"Good idea. Keep me posted."

"Will do."

Before Dan could make another call, the phone rang. It was Charlie Watkins.

"Dan, the passenger in the car was not Mrs. Kerr. We have a positive ID. Her name is Laura Bridgewater. She was pronounced dead at the scene."

Anger, confusion, regret, and sadness all pinged in Dan's mind as he reeled at this latest bad news. He thanked Charlie and hung up. He turned to Rosalina and told her in a stunned whisper, his face ashen, "The passenger was not Elaine. It was Laura Bridgewater, my employee. Why didn't I fire her when I had the chance? Now she's dead thanks to Pup's carelessness. A promising young life wasted."

Rosalina reached for him. "Dan, you can't blame yourself. It was a tragic accident. Leave it at that. It serves no purpose to assign blame. I wonder if Elaine even knows it happened. We should call her."

Dan reluctantly picked up the phone again. One of the boys answered. "Hi, Chase, this is Uncle Chip. Could I speak with your mother?"

"Sure. Hold on."

"Hello?"

"Hi, Elaine. It's Dan. I'm sorry to tell you this, but Pup has been involved in a car accident. He's being sent to Boston for further evaluation."

"Why didn't the hospital call me? How did you find out?"

"A friend of mine who's a cop called me from the scene."

"You said John's being sent to Boston? It must be pretty bad."

"It is. The three of us should go to Boston in the morning. We'll leave early to avoid the rush. Rosie and I will pick you up at six-thirty."

"Ok. I can't believe this. Please let me know if you hear anything else."

"I will. Good night, Elaine. Try to get some sleep."

Dan didn't have the heart to tell her about Laura. He needed time to find the words to break it to her as gently as possible.

Dan, Rosalina, and Elaine left early the next morning for the hospital in Boston. All during the drive, Dan couldn't calm his mind, no matter how hard he tried. Concern about Pup's condition and remorse over Laura's death had prevented him from sleeping and clouded his thinking. The tension in the car was palpable. Rosalina and Elaine said little while Dan tried to concentrate on driving, to remain focused even though his mind replayed the conversation with Charlie Watkins over and over.

Pup had been admitted to the ICU, so visits were restricted. Elaine went in alone while Dan and Rosalina sipped wretched hospital coffee in the family waiting room. When Elaine returned a half hour later, she was composed despite her pallor and obvious lack of sleep. "John is in a medically induced coma," she told Dan and Rosalina. "His vital signs are good, and he will live."

Dan breathed an audible sigh of relief as did Rosalina. "However," Elaine continued, "His condition is grave but stable. I spoke with his nurse, but she had just come on duty and hadn't read the night nurse's notes so she couldn't tell me a great deal. She did say that the doctor would be in to see John around eight o'clock. I need coffee."

Dan fetched coffee for his sister-in-law and then went to Pup's cubicle. As much as he had tried to steel himself, Dan was still taken aback by all the wires and monitors that surrounded Pup's bed. The incessant beeping of the monitors annoyed Dan, but he couldn't stop himself from glancing at the heart monitor and its hypnotic tracing of Pup's heart rate. To his inexperienced eye, Pup seemed to be holding his own.

Again, conflicting emotions swirled in Dan. One part of him wanted to slap his brother senseless even though another part of him wanted to take Pup into his arms and just hold him. Dan stared at the livid bruises that covered Pup's face and the large laceration on his forehead. Pup's mouth was a solid line, the lips clamped shut. The iv pole to the left of the bed mechanically dripped medication into Pup's veins. There was already a bruise where the needle punctured the skin.

When Dan returned to the waiting room, he saw Rosalina comforting a distraught Elaine. The enormity of what had happened had struck Elaine. She sobbed pitifully in Rosalina's arms. Dan didn't know how to react to the scene before him, so he sat and picked up a magazine and flipped mindlessly through it.

The doctor arrived and briefed the family. "Mr. Kerr has sustained a head injury, but we are still not sure of its severity," intoned the doctor. "From what we can see, he also fractured some vertebrae which means he's paralyzed from the waist down. We can't tell just yet what his mental status will be. That will be determined when we slowly awaken him from the coma. That's all I can tell you right now."

"Will my brother recover from the head injury?" inquired Dan.

"We have not determined the full extent of the head trauma. We're still running tests."

"When will you know?"

The doctor answered patiently, "We could know as early as tonight. The plan is to do as many scans as possible today. If the radiologist can read the early scans today, we'll have a pretty good idea of the extent of the head trauma."

The family thanked the doctor and left. The drive home was quiet. Dan, Rosalina, and Elaine were all exhausted, worn out from the shock of the upheaval in their lives. When he got home, Dan called Bridy to update her on Pup's condition. She was calm and ready to take charge as the family spokesperson, thus relieving Dan of that responsibility.

"Dad's anxious, but otherwise ok," she informed Dan. "It would be good though if you could come over and tell him what you told me." Dan agreed and promised to visit after he napped that afternoon. The only silver lining, thought Dan, was that he didn't have to tell his mother that her oldest son would never walk again.

Chapter 15

Dan agonized over how to tell Elaine about Laura for he had not yet done so. He didn't want to call her. A phone call would not be appropriate for so sensitive a subject. He would have to meet her in person, but where? Finally, he decided to invite her over for dinner so Rosalina would be there to help Dan deliver the news and help Elaine absorb the painful truth about her husband.

Dan knew he had to get back to the office, which was in almost total chaos, between reporters trying to cover the biggest local story of their careers while grieving the death of one on their own. Rachel had reported to Dan that a good many of the staff were angry with Pup and by extension Dan since Laura had been popular and well respected at the *Clarion*.

Rachel also told Dan that she had incurred the wrath of the acting mayor when she refused to give him Dan's home phone number. She told him in no uncertain terms to go to hell, that Dan was grieving also and deserved his privacy. Dan smiled at Rachel's unswerving loyalty. She would tell off anyone foolish enough to cross her. But Dan was the boss, and he should be there to try to organize the staff and put out the numerous brush fires that angry employees had started.

Once back there, he holed up in his office to attend to a personal and difficult task: he needed to write a letter to Laura's parents. He wanted to convey to them how sorry he was, not only for the conduct of his brother but also for his own regrets about Laura's death. Despite his many years in the business, Dan found that words eluded him as he stared at the computer screen, his mind a complete blank. Rachel was standing sentinel, and he knew no one would get past her, no matter how urgent the errand. No one would be able to interrupt him. Nevertheless, Dan struggled to complete even a sentence. His concern about Elaine and the news he had yet to give her, had clouded his thinking and erased every semblance of coherent thought.

The phone startled him when it rang. A nearly hysterical Elaine told him that a reporter had called and asked if she had any comment about her husband's passenger that evening. Dan was furious that one his reporters would be so callous as to make such a call, but he was also furious with himself for neglecting to tell Elaine sooner. Dan demanded the name of the reporter whom he vowed to fire as soon as he finished talking to Elaine. Between sobs and gasps, Elaine asked if Dan had any knowledge of Pup's relationship with Laura. Dan told his now hyperventilating sister-in-law that he had suspected an affair between Pup and Laura, but he had no solid evidence. This was only partly true, and Dan felt terrible that he couldn't come out and tell Elaine the truth. His heart swelled with pity for this poor woman, but some unknowable constraint prevented him from being totally honest. Inwardly he cursed his innate loyalty to his brother, the family renegade who had caused so much trouble.

Dan placated Elaine as best he could and promised to talk to her later. Abandoning the computer, he reached for a pen and a pad of paper hoping the old-fashioned way of expressing condolences would stimulate his mind. He made a list of all the words he thought he should use, and this did help to get his creative juices flowing. His mind drifted back to his high school days when his teachers would say to just write whatever comes into your head. You can always fix it later. Slowly, he managed to write a couple of paragraphs, inadequate as he felt they were. But he had something.

Dan abandoned the task since he felt he was not getting anywhere. He heaved himself up from his desk and strode into the newsroom where reporters were busy composing stories and racing to make deadlines. Several looked up as he passed them, but he headed straight to the oaf who had called Elaine. In one swift gesture, Dan flung the man's chair around, nearly upending it. The startled reporter stared up at Dan, a look of fear etched on his face.

Dan went nose to nose with the man. "You have ten minutes to clean out your desk and get the hell out of here. You're fired. How dare you be so obtuse and crass as to call the mayor's wife. Your conduct was unprofessional and totally lacking in compassion. If you're not gone in ten minutes, I'll have to police escort you out." Then turning to the rest of the people in the room, Dan yelled, "That goes for the rest of you also. You are to use discretion and tact when reporting on this story. Anything less will result in your termination. Do I make myself clear?"

No one spoke as they stared open mouthed at their ordinarily affable boss who stalked past them back to his office, slammed the door, and flung his coffee cup against the wall. All the noise alarmed Rachel who tentatively opened the door. "Are you all right, Mr. Kerr?"

Dan, exhausted and panting, looked up. "No, Rachel. I'm not all right. I think I should quit right now. I just fired Cooper for unprofessional conduct. I was out of control in front of most of the staff. How can I ever get their respect back? My life is in a shambles. All of this is my brother's fault. Every bit of it. What do I do now?"

Rachel said quietly, "Mr. Kerr, you need to take some time off. You have suffered a family tragedy which you must deal with. You've also suffered the personal loss of a member of the staff. There is no answer as to how to rectify the situation. This is a newspaper, and these people are doing their jobs under very difficult circumstances. They need you also. You cannot help anyone in your present state. Go home and rest. You're going on vacation, so take a few extra days to sort out the situation. Quitting now is the worst thing you could do. There are plenty of people here who can make sure the paper functions. Everyone knows who the real boss is anyway." This last remark was delivered with a smirk which made Dan smile. He knew his plain-spoken secretary was right. He needed time to think and decompress. That could not be done in the pressure cooker atmosphere of the paper. With that, he thanked Rachel, gathered up his half-written letter to the Bridgewaters, and exited via the back door.

Dan did not go home, instead he went to see Elaine. She greeted him cordially, but the boys were silently hostile and hardly acknowledged Dan. Elaine invited Dan into the den and after mixing two drinks she talked. "I'm sorry for the way I acted on the phone, Dan. I'm not only upset with the situation, but especially for the effect it's having on the boys. Both refuse to see their father. They want nothing to do with him."

"I'm sorry that Pup has caused all this trouble for you and the boys, Elaine. I wish there was something I could do to make it right."

"This is not the first time I've dealt with this. John has a long history of being with other women. I've suspected for some time that he's being seeing someone on the side, but I didn't connect it to the reporter. I thought she was too young for John. Turns out I was wrong. The first time was when we were still living in Texas. John swore he would never see any other women, but he was unable to keep that promise."

"Why did you stay with him?"

Elaine sighed and was silent for a long moment. "I stayed because I wanted the boys to have a real home with a mother and a father. Moving here was good since your family is so close to each other. I'm glad that the boys have had a chance to see a real family and how they act. I'm also glad that the family was able to accept me, a Texan." She gave a small laugh. "I feel comfortable here. This is my home and the boys' home also. I've forgiven John in the past and I will forgive him again. I'm sure this will put an end to this behavior. It's too bad it took such an unfortunate event to make John see the light, so to speak."

As Dan listened, he realized what a remarkable woman Elaine was. She was willing to forgive her philandering husband for the sake of her children. Many other women would not have tolerated such behavior, much less forgiven their spouse for his indiscretions. Pup did not deserve such an incredible woman.

"Don't misunderstand me," Elaine continued. "I could kill him for what he's done to the boys and me and the entire family.

I learned long ago that John needs his ego stroked constantly. He's a weak person despite his bravado and bluff and bluster. Having women on the side is one way that he chose to validate himself. He's basically a good man. He's a hard worker and he has always done everything to give the boys and me the best life possible. For that I thank him. Now things will be different. But in the end, John will be the one who will suffer the most. His reputation, which he cherished, is shot to hell. He will never be the mayor again, no matter how much people like him. He likely will face charges since he was responsible for another person's death. I try not to think about this, but I'm sure he will have to pay somehow. I need to stand by him because just about everyone else will abandon him."

Dan felt his anger well up again. "I also could kill him for what he's done. Pup has always caused trouble in one way or another. He usually got away with things at home because he was my mother's favorite. So, he thought he could do whatever he wanted without any consequences. Everybody loved him because of his gregarious personality so people were willing to overlook a lot. Hence, Pup thought he was a golden boy who could do whatever he wanted. If someone called him on something, Pup could charm his way out of trouble. That's how he's lived his life. Until now."

"Another drink, Dan? I'm glad we had this talk. Thank you for listening and not judging. I hope I have the support of the rest of the family. I really need it."

Dan took Elaine's hand. "I'll pass on the drink, but I can assure you that you will always have me in your corner. I'm also glad that we spoke. Would you and the boys like to come to dinner tonight? Rosie and I would love to have you."

"Thank you. I'll come. I don't know about the boys. They're pretty angry at the world right now. What time?"

"Six. See you then."

Dan returned to his office through the front door. Rachel was leaving for the day and gave a little scream of surprise when she saw him. "I thought I told you to go home and stay there."

"I had to come back to finish some important business. I now feel able to face whatever is ahead of me. I just spoke with my brother's wife. She's absolutely amazing, almost as amazing as you. I should hire her to work with you."

Arms akimbo, Rachel retorted, "That will be the day. Do what you have to do and go home. I don't want to see you tomorrow or the day after. You hear me?"

"Yes, Mom. I promise not to work too long."

Dan sat at his desk and wrote a heartfelt letter of condolence to Laura's parents. He snapped out the light to his office and went home to his wife.

Dan and Rosalina, Elaine, Mr. Kerr, Bridy, and the Salinas all had dinner at the Kerr family home that night. Mrs. Salina made two pans of lasagna and Salina brought plenty of his homemade wine. The occasion might have been festive if not for the gravity of the situation involving Pup. Dan felt a stab of guilt that he had not spoken to his father since the accident. He would have to make some time to speak privately with him. Since the Salinas were like family, everyone present felt they could speak freely.

Bridy had called all the siblings and given them the details. She recalled that the reactions were typical of each individual. Mimi was furious at first then resigned. Cissy railed on about Pup and how he was a disgrace to the family and vowed never to speak to him again. Gabby was shocked but convinced that everything would be all right in the end. Biddy just wrote the whole incident off as typical Pup. "So, everybody knows," reported Bridy.

Dan thought about how much drama this family had endured over the years. Sometimes he wondered if the family had been cursed in the way of a Greek tragedy. He knew this was not the case, but he groped for an explanation as to why one family had to cope with so much heartache. Even Mrs. Salina, seldom at a loss for words, just shook her head sadly.

The next day, Elaine called to say that Pup had begun to speak as the doctors slowly awakened him. But later that day the good news was offset when Charlie Watkins called Dan to tell him that the police were going to charge Pup with vehicular homicide in the death of Laura Bridgewater. Pup would be arraigned at his bedside as soon as he was fully conscious.

"We had to wait until we were sure the mayor was going to live before we could officially charge him," Charlie explained. Dan took the news calmly. It was not that much of a surprise. Now Dan would have to discuss Pup's defense with Elaine, who would have to hire a lawyer.

On the way home that night, Dan swung by his office to pick up his diary. The tattered notebook had lain in Dan's top drawer for two months. Now Dan felt that he needed to once again find solace in reading about an uncomplicated time of his life. "I need to read this so don't give me any crap, ok?" He admonished Rosalina.

His wife raised her hands in surrender. "None from me."

Dan and Rosalina had to make a decision about the cruise. Both still wanted to go but felt guilty given Pup's situation. They had to decide soon since the cruise was in two weeks. Mr. Kerr unwittingly made the decision for them. Dan had finally found the chance to talk to his father privately a few days after the lasagna dinner. Mr. Kerr had always been philosophical about life's problems, and he hadn't changed. "Dad," said Dan. "I'm sorry that I didn't speak to your sooner, but the office is in chaos and trips to Boston to see Pup have put a serious dent in my free time."

"Don't worry about it. Life happens. You don't need to come running over here every time there's a crisis, but I do like your visits, don't get me wrong."

"I like our one-on-one chats also. How are you feeling about Pup?"

Mr. Kerr gathered his thoughts. "Frankly, I'm not surprised. Trouble has followed Pup his entire life, and this is certainly the worst ever. I'm really sorry that a young woman had to lose her life because of Pup. Had he been seeing this woman, do you know?"

"I'm not absolutely certain, but I think so. Several months ago, I became suspicious, and I asked Pup point blank. He told me in effect to mind my own business. Then I asked Laura who told me pretty much the same thing. My plan had been to fire Laura but instead I reassigned her, thinking foolishly that if she didn't cover city hall, she would end whatever relationship she had with Pup. I should have fired her, but I didn't. Now I'm agonizing over her death. It's awful, Dad. I can't sleep or concentrate at work. My life is a mess."

"At least you will have a chance to get away soon."

"Rosie and I are trying to decide whether or not to take the cruise."

"Of course you should take the cruise. Pup will live, so you don't have to worry about that. There's absolutely nothing you can do now about the young woman's death. You need to concentrate on your own life. Besides, the trip is for Rosalina. Do you want to take that away from her?"

"No, of course not. What will my sisters think if I take off and ignore another Kerr family crisis?"

"Who cares what they think? You've your own life to live. You paid a lot of money for this trip. My advice is to go. I would say the same to any of your sisters."

"Thanks, Dad. I'm glad we talked. I feel a lot better."

Dan knew it was now incumbent upon him to make things right at work. He and the staff had been co-existing under a flimsy cease fire, but that had to change. Dan knew he was sitting on a powder keg which only he could defuse. He spent several hours writing a memo to give to each person at the paper. After several drafts, he gave up. He would have to call a staff meeting and speak to the group as a whole and let them air their own grievances. It would be hard, but it had to be done.

Dan put a notice in everyone's mailbox announcing an all staff meeting for the next day at nine. That night he tossed and turned trying to decide exactly what he could say to these people that would have any kind of impact. The circumstances were so extraordinary that Dan was at a loss as to how to express how he was feeling let alone try to acknowledge the feelings of his employees. He scrawled a few words on his legal pad reasoning that if Abraham Lincoln could write the Gettysburg Address on the back of an envelope, he could find the right words to help his staff, but he doubted what he wrote would ever be remembered by anyone.

The conference room was packed but subdued. People sipped coffee and waited to hear what Dan had to say. At precisely nine o'clock Dan stepped behind the podium, adjusted the microphone, and said, "Good morning. Let me begin by apologizing to all of you for my behavior the other day. The events of recent days have left me frazzled and short tempered. I grieve for Laura as I know all of you do. Her death has been a cruel blow to the Clarion family. We all know that Laura was a consummate professional who loved her work, and it showed in its quality. Despite our heavy hearts, we must still come together to get the work done. All of you have done an extraordinary job covering the events surrounding Laura's death. We must continue to do so even though the nature of the work compounds our pain. Does anyone have any questions?"

Predictably enough, Sutcliffe stood and fired his question. "Will the editorial board back a recall petition for the mayor? He is unfit to serve and should be removed from office."

Dan countered, "That is a decision that must be reached through a consensus of the board and the managing editor. It not a step to be taken lightly."

Sutcliffe continued. "Would you support a recall or will loyalty to your brother override the board's decision?"

Dan wanted nothing more than to leap across the podium and take Sutcliffe by the throat. He knew the editor was baiting him, trying to show him up before the entire staff. Dan took a deep breath to try to keep his voice under control. "I make no apologies for the actions of the mayor, nor do I defend him as my brother. We've had this conversation many times and my position has not changed. You, of all people, should be aware of that by now, Sutcliffe."

Another hand went up. "Is the paper going to do anything for Laura's family?"

"Such as?"

"A memorial or some kind of recognition for her?"

"I wrote a letter of condolence to the Bridgewater family. I don't know what else we could do. We can't rename the paper for her."

A ripple of anger hummed through the conference room. "That was uncalled for, Dan," a voice in the crowd said.

Dan had always ascribed to the expression, 'Don't let them see you sweat,' but now he was sweating and losing his grip. Several people were now leaving the meeting and casting angry glances at Dan. "I am open to suggestions, if anyone has any." With that, Dan had no choice but to end the meeting.

"I'm sorry to say this, but you blew it, Mr. Kerr," his ever-faithful secretary Rachel announced when Dan returned to his office. He ignored her and slammed the door. He cursed Pup, Laura, Sutcliffe, the *Clarion*, heaven, and hell. Never in his life had Dan felt so alone and defeated. He had made an ass of himself in front of the people he was supposed to lead. How would he ever be able to reclaim their respect and trust? Should he just resign? Call another meeting? Write an apologetic memo? What?

A light tap at his door woke him from his stupor. Rachel poked her head in. "May I come in?"

"Yes. You have to help me, Rachel. This is an impossible situation. I don't have a clue what to do. I've gotten myself in over my head and I'm drowning."

"Mr. Kerr, you must acknowledge that everyone here is grieving, and everyone handles grief in a different way. These people need to talk, but they can't because they have work to do. But you need to find a way to help them to at least deal with their grief. If you don't eventually all hell will break loose. It's already started."

"What do you suggest?"

"Get a professional in here, someone who isn't an employee and can see the situation objectively. At least make that person available and then each person can decide whether to talk or not. You can't do it. You're too deeply involved."

"Do they blame me for what my brother did?"

"Some do, but not all. But most are angry at the mayor and, since he's your brother, it follows that they are angry at you as well. I can call some agencies and arrange to get someone here to help. It's a small step, but it is a step."

"Fine. Do that. Can you think of anything else? My mind is a complete blank. And while you're at it, hire a hit man to kill Sutcliffe."

Rachel looked at Dan over her glasses. "Mr. Kerr. Uncalled for again."

"Sorry. I'm losing it more and more every minute."

"You should be the first in line when the counselor gets here."

"I will be."

The next morning the editorial board held its weekly meeting. Dan arrived before anyone else, determined to look each editor in the eye as he entered the room. He wanted to send a clear signal that no insubordination would be tolerated. Dan was more than ready to fire anyone who crossed the line. The group that entered was subdued and businesslike. In journalistic terms, the accident was old news, but the fate of the mayor was a hot topic that could not be avoided. Sutcliffe proposed that the *Clarion* make its position clear by calling for the mayor to resign or face a recall election. Dan had no objection to this stance and the board voted unanimously to devote the Thursday editorial to this issue.

Several other local stories were bandied about as was the board's custom. All went smoothly and without rancor. Dan felt his pent-up rage abate as the board calmly went about its business. Before the conclusion of the meeting, Dan announced that two grief counselors would be available later that day to talk to any staff members who were interested. Murmurs of assent rippled across the table. As he stood, an editor named Donovan asked Dan if he planned to speak to a counselor. "You should, Dan. You really need to vent. Otherwise, you might end up killing Sutcliffe. Where would the *Clarion* be then?"

Dan smiled and relaxed. He had never expected any kind of support from anyone on the editorial board. His relationship with them at been prickly at best. This sudden goodwill caught him totally off guard. Even Sutcliffe smiled, a rare event in itself. Slow down, thought Dan. Don't take this as a change of heart on the part of the board. This was likely just a peace offering that could be withdrawn at any time. But it was something, and Dan was willing to accept it, however temporary it might be.

Dan and Rosalina left for the cruise two days later. Rachel had assured Dan that she would take care of everything in his absence. Dan wondered if he and Rachel should change places. She could run the organization as effectively as any CEO. He could retire and cruise around the world. Thoughts like that could only be banished by taking a long and relaxing vacation. Dan took the diary along and read it faithfully cover to cover several times. He came across what he had written as Pup prepared to leave to join the Marines.

We had a family party for Pup. Mum cooked roast beef, Pup's favorite, along with boiled potatoes, green beans, and cake for dessert. The Salinas were invited and Mrs. Salina made lasagna. I was hoping Angelina would come, but only Mr. and Mrs. Salina came. Both sets of grandparents were there also. We had a lot of laughs, but I was kind of sad and I know Mum was as well. Dad had a little too much of Salina's homemade wine and he was constantly talking about what he did during the war and how proud he was of Pup, who was following in his footsteps. If we didn't have company, I think Mum would have let him have it. He's been reminding her constantly that what Pup is doing is honorable and she should be proud of him. Mum isn't listening. I think all she sees is her oldest son leaving and perhaps never coming back.

We all chipped in and bought Pup a round trip ticket home when he finishes his basic training. That will be at the end of August or early September. I can't wait till then.

Pup left today. Dad drove him to the train station. Mum didn't want to go. She's really having a hard time with Pup's leaving. We all watched from the front yard along with the grandparents and most of the neighbors. I'm still hoping the Marines will tell Pup that they don't need him, that they have enough guys joining. I know that won't happen, but I can dream. Grammy could tell I was sad. She came and put her arm around me.

"You know," she said. "I felt the same way when your uncle went off to the service. It was awful because he was going into the Second World War. At least now there is no war. Pup could end up some place like Paris or Rome."

Paris and Rome were just places on the map to me. Pup would still be a long way from home.

"Cheer up, Chip. Pup will be all right. Some day you will leave, either for the service or college. Mimi left to get married. Everyone grows up and moves on. Pup will come back, and we'll all be very proud of the man he will become."

Dan considered this last entry from the diary for a long time. So much had happened since the time that Pup left for the Marines. Any illusions that Dan had about Pup had long been dispelled. In a moment of sudden clarity Dan knew he had to accept the family and Pup as they were not as he wanted them to be. He sighed and took a long swallow of his wine, heaved himself up, and headed to the balcony.

"Where are you going?" Rosalina asked.

"Onto the balcony for some fresh air." Then Dan took one last look at his faded, corrugated journal before he flung the diary into the midnight blue waters of the Caribbean Sea and watched as it receded into the night to the low rumble of distant thunder.

Acknowledgments

This manuscript has become a book with the indispensable assistance of many people. I extend my heartfelt thanks to Eileen O'Finlan for her example of what a dedicated writer should be. My thanks also to the writing group: Lee Baldarelli, Janice Hitzhusen, Jim Pease, Pam Reponen, Cindy Shinette, and Rebecca Southwick who showed me that creation doesn't have to be drudgery; it can be fun. To Elizabeth Beliveau, a truly gifted artist who creates from the soul. To Jessica Meltzer, publisher pre-eminent, whose patience knows no bounds, and whose hard work and good humor spur this author to reach back for her best.